BALL

BALL

stories by

TARA ISON

SOFT SKULL PRESS
An Imprint of Counterpoint
Berkeley

Also By Tara Ison

A Child Out of Alcatraz

The List

Rockaway

Reeling Through Life

Library of Congress Cataloging-in-Publication Data

Ison, Tara.
[Short stories. Selections]
Ball : stories / Tara Ison.
    pages ; cm
ISBN 978-1-59376-622-1
I. Title.
PS3559.566A6 2015
813›.54—dc23
2015011962

Cover design by Kelly Winton
Interior design by Domini Dragoone
Author photo © Michael Powers

Soft Skull Press
An Imprint of COUNTERPOINT
2560 Ninth Street, Suite 318
Berkeley, CA 94710
www.softskull.com

Printed in the United States of America
Distributed by Publishers Group West

10 9 8 7 6 5 4 3 2 1

for Theda

CONTENTS

CACTUS

I haven't left the apartment in nine months. My current boy-friend, Paul, has tried. He's tried to lure me outside with tick-ets to the Hollywood Bowl or the Greek, lobster dinners on the Santa Monica Pier, a drive to the outlet mall in Camarillo for shoes. He combs *LA Weekly* in search of compelling events. He seeks to entice me with unmuggy, azure-skied days, with dove-gray rain days, with his twilight-walk-on-the-beach idea of romance. He brought me a kite, a neon-lime rhombus with an optimistic mile of spooled nylon string, and proposed Laguna Beach. He bought me a pair of rollerblades, then he bought me a Jet Ski. Actually, his parents bought it, for both of us. But his parents have always liked me. Paul thinks going outside will be good for me, scrub off dull cells of skin, freshen my blood, inspire bloom. You need some sun, he says hopefully, light and fresh air.

A change of atmosphere. You're pale. You need to go outside. He talks about the necessary vitamin D absorption from ultraviolet rays. He cajoles, pleads, pouts, but in the end I give him shopping lists, and he comes back with everything I've asked for.

I don't need to go outside. My computer is right there on my desk, and my work, mail, contact, come to me. Light and sky, a vertical swatch of the Hollywood Hills, all find me through the faux-bay window in the living room. I can plant myself safely in the window seat I rigged up and look out, see pavement, Laurel Avenue, cars, the street cleaner on Tuesday mornings, a sleeping ceramic child and the ugly, treacherous, stolen cactus in our small plot of front yard. Paul has refused to water the cactus, thinking that will get me to rise, but I remind him: It's a *cactus*. Go on, withhold water. It'll just mock us. It'll outlive us both. Just try to master it, and, more likely, you'll be the one to get hurt.

This cactus stabbed me once, so I know what I'm talking about.

JOSH, MY FORMER boyfriend, dug the cactus out of the ground in front of me on our only trip to the Mojave Desert. He had a job leading overnight hiking excursions for junior high and high school kids. He had a stock of whistles and white cotton French Foreign Legion–style caps. He'd drive a herd of bored, sweating students out to places like Death Valley, Anza-Borrego, Indian Canyon, in a renovated bus donated by the L.A.

City School District, and explain how crashing tectonic plates thrust up the mountains and granite shafts, how melting glaciers once filled the basins with lakes, about global warming patterns and elevation and evolving ecosystems, how the water burrowed itself deeper underground as if looking to hide while harsh, parching winds swept soil into dunes. He showed them bedrock worn down and exposed like picked-clean bones. He taught them about the Pleistocene Pinto people, and the Serrano Indians who lived on pinyon nuts, cactus fruit, and mesquite beans, wove sandals and baskets from the shredded, curly fibers of Mojave yucca, and left behind their pottery and rock paintings. He explained how explorers a hundred years ago dammed up the last trickles of water, plundered the desert for gold, and left a honeycomb of mines. He pointed out arroyos, playas, and alluvial fans baked down to dust, the stump of a basalt volcano, aplite and gneiss glinting in the sun. At dusk he showed them emerging kangaroo rats and desert iguanas and burrowing owls, explained how roadrunners get all the moisture they need from the bodily fluids of reptiles, insects, and rodents they eat, taught them how every desert animal has adapted in body shape or metabolism or special skill to hang on to its place as predator or prey. At night he and his students would all lie in their mummy bags under the black celestial dome, undimmed by any fake municipal glow, and watch the elliptic path of the planets, the zodiacal chase of stars. It's the vastness of it all, he would always tell them, me, sounding drug-fried or stupid, neither of which he is. His favorite word, *vast*—vast desert, landscape, atmosphere, universe, space. Earth: a core of rock, a crumbled mantle, a thin forsaken crust, and a mere us between it and the vast and boundless sky. He said it was the vastness that got to them every time, what they succumbed to, the letting go of small things, but I know what got to them was him. I pictured the cynical, trooping teenagers rolling their eyes, elbowing each other, then finally cracking smiles. I pictured them losing their cool urban sheaths and succumbing to his desert varnish, his energized mirage, his pulse. Succumbing to this oasis of a person. He said it was the vastness that got to them, but I know that's what got to *him*, rooted him, somehow made him feel peace. I didn't get it. All that quiet just sounded lonely to me. The idea of succumbing to all that space made me feel aimless and lost. I could never understand why he'd want to feel so insignificant.

I USED TO watch him pack for his trips. He'd squeeze one spare everything into a small duffel bag and reel off the desert's vast beauties he couldn't wait to get back to, while in my head I listed ways he might get hurt. A blistering third-degree burn, despite the sunblock. Heatstroke, despite the cap. The skull-splitting fall from a rock. A flash flood while he slept. In my mind he'd go to retrieve a student who'd wandered into a forbidden, abandoned mine, only to have it collapse on top of him in a thundering billow of rock. He always packed a topographic map and compass, but I suspected he'd get lost one day in the pirouetting cactus–boulder–cow skull, cactus–boulder–cow-skull backdrop of the cartoon Southwest. I'd watch him load the bus with plastic five-gallon barrels of water—*I want you guys guzzling two gallons per person per day*, I'd hear him warn students on the phone in his teacher's voice, *you gotta replace that sweat!*—and think: evaporation, dehydration. I pictured him desperately sucking a chunk of cactus. I pictured him writhing with heat cramp. He always packed a shovel, in case the bus got mired in sand, and I'd picture a fresh-dug desert grave, his body wrapped in the shiny green Hefty bags he took along for trash and already melting into his skin in the sun. He had a cooler the size of a steamer trunk packed with food and bricks of ice, and I'd think: starvation, botulism. The first aid kit didn't reassure me; it confirmed my fears. There were desert tarantulas and desert snakes, and I'd watch him sharpen his jackknife and scissors and imagine him coming back in a limp, drained stagger, his body marked with a cross where some student had X'd over a fanged puncture to suck out and spit the poison from his blood. Every time he came home, a mere him, hair burned a lighter blond, his fruit-leather skin covered in a gritty sweat and his nape bright as tomato from having loaned his neck-flap cap to a student too arrogant to bring his own, I'd busy myself with a special dinner, something cool with mint and cucumber, draw him a tepid bath, bustle and fuss all to avoid a hysteric relief at having him return okay. Each time he came back unhurt I stockpiled the fear, carried it over to the next time, weighed the increase of odds that meant nothing bad had happened yet and so next time, of course, it would.

When we were first together, he'd always asked me to go along. When we were first together I wasn't scared at all, and I always shrugged and said *No, I don't feel like it, I'm not much of an outdoors person, You go, we're not joined at the hip, You go, we're going to grow old together, right?, plenty of time, You go, we don't have to do everything together, we don't have to share all the same interests, right?* Plus the lack of privacy, the adolescent throng, the harsh and lunar-sounding landscape, the herding and the rules—*bag up and ziplock your toilet paper, you guys, leave no trace!*—always made it sound more like work than play. And I didn't want to be part of his work, just one more thing he had to pack and take along. I wanted to carry more weight than that. But then after a while I thought maybe if it was just us two. I wasn't seeing him that much. He was being successful and busy at his job, scheduling extra excursions. *That's what's so great about you, Holly*, he'd say to me, leaving, *You're so independent.* He was away a lot of weekends, then a lot of weekdays, too, and getting an edgy, cramped look sometimes when he was home. So I finally suggested it, my going with him and just us two, and he wanted to know why I'd changed my mind. He wanted to know what I possibly thought

I'd get out of it. *You're not very adaptable, Holly,* he mumbled into my neck one night over the whir of the window fan. And I said *See? That's the point, I don't understand the appeal. This will expand my horizon.* But when I said that I realized it was his horizon that worried me; his was getting too big and far away for me to be more than a speck in it. A mere me. I was a dot on his landscape, and I wanted to be a vast and boundless thing for him. I wanted him to succumb to me. I went to the outlet mall and bought hiking boots, a special sunscreen with alpha hydroxy. But by that time I wasn't just worried, I was also getting scared, for him, and he had stopped asking me to go.

Then one bland, humid Friday morning last April, the phone rang with someone telling me that weekend's excursion to Joshua Tree was called off due to an outbreak of flu at some East L.A. junior high. Josh was outside loading the bus and, when I told him, got his edgy, penned-up animal look, the one that says *let me out.*

Shit, he said. He sighed, regarded the bus a moment. Then he turned back to me. Okay, let's go. We'll go, just us two.

Now? I said.

I'm packed up. I have the permit. It's April. I can't stay here all weekend, he said, gesturing at the street and pavement. He had refused to plant grass on our little front plot, saying lawn in Los Angeles was an environmental insult. I'd thought maybe just a rose bush would be nice, but instead we had a found-rock garden.

We'd spot lost-looking rocks in alleys or streets, bring them home. At first I'd thought it was fun, kitschy, but today the rocks just looked forced. Horns honked down on Sunset Boulevard; there was a siren's rise and ebb, a jet, a helicopter's anxious drone, the hot gasp of wetted city cement, the smell of exhaust.

What's the problem, Holly? he said. You said you wanted to go.

I saw us going back inside the apartment where it was safe and where he didn't want to be, saw spending a weekend together, just us two, with four walls and a roof and a window unit that cooled and filtered air. Then I saw him saying *I'll go, I'll just go myself*, and then going by himself. Leaving me in favor of all those dangers. Wandering off and never coming back. I saw the snake venom coursing through and no one ready with a knife; I saw him dead from exposure and no one there to dig his grave. I saw turkey vultures swooping in to pick his bones clean. This wasn't him wanting to *leave* me, I realized with relief; this was him *needing* me. This was him not wanting to get hurt, not wanting to be alone, not wanting to let go. Wanting to let me in to fill up all his precious space.

I went inside and put on my boots and sunblock. We transferred mummy bags and shovel and cooler and first aid kit and wheelbarrow and gallons of water from the school bus to his truck, left Hollywood, and drove a few hours east from Los Angeles along the 10, where the world went dull and beige, full of highway and dirt without nap, tired motels and shopping malls and hamburger drive-thrus collapsed at the foot of mountains as if dumped off cliffs. Then, somewhere beyond the turnoff for Palm Springs, higher and higher up and farther on Route 62, the dunnish air cleared and the Mojave Desert slowly unrolled into lucid bloom. Magentas, lemons, purples, oranges, whites, from the horizon to us, a sudden extravagance, and the wind-snap of sage, nectar, honest rock, succulent air.

See? he said. April.

I pictured it all dead, I said.

It's never dead. It looks dead in fall and winter, sometimes, when a lot of it's dormant. But then it all explodes.

I took off my boots and hung my feet out the window, so my toes could breathe. I leaned back against him, and he put his arm around me, poked his nose in my ear. He kissed my throat and said, See?

Yes, I said.

No, look, a Joshua tree, he said, pointing.

We were passing a lanky, trunked thing, its branches out-stretched in stiff torsion, each one ending in a tuft of spines. We passed another one, then three.

Joshua trees, he said. This is the only place in the world they live. And they live hundreds of years. The Mormons called them that. They drove out in their wagons to California and suddenly saw all of these and said they looked like Joshua, his arms up, welcoming them to the Promised Land.

He slowed the truck. The tree didn't look like a welcoming prophet to me. Its trunk was covered in spikes scaled like a chain mail of daggers. The raised branch-arms looked deformed. It looked like an armored soldier with boiling oil poured down his back, caught in the first moment of panicked, agonized cringe.

We passed more, and then many, and then they were everywhere. It was a whole field of trapped and seared Joshuas trying desperately to grip the sky, shaking twisted, crippled fists at God.

WE STOPPED AT the Oasis Visitor Center in Twentynine Palms. Josh registered the truck at the backcountry board while I examined glass jars of jewel-colored cactus marmalades, cactus pickles, cactus candy. The labels showed a thorny cactus fruit split in half, revealing tender, pulpy insides. I bought granola bars and another half-liter bottle of water and leafed through a book called *Common Cacti of the Southwest*.

Look, I said to him, showing. I'm learning all about cacti. We should get this.

Holly, he said. He took the book from me and put it back. You're here. You don't need a book to *show* you here.

All right, you teach me.

Just be patient. He smiled at me as I tore the wrapper off a chocolate chip granola bar and ate it. You have to be patient in the desert, Holly. Give it up.

Before leaving, we walked up close to a smallish Joshua tree. A woodpecker rapped at a branch. Josh showed me wrens nesting in the tree's topmost spines and thumbnail moths collecting pollen from the blossom clusters, laying eggs. He nudged a toppled, decaying limb with his foot; a kangaroo rat scuttled away, and termites surged.

It's the perfect ecosystem, he said in his teacher's voice. All in itself. The living tree is food and home for birds and insects and rodents. And then even when it's dead, it's food and home. The energy just keeps cycling, being transformed. There's life everywhere, if you just look for it.

Oh, God, I said, ducking. In front of me was a fat lizard impaled on a spike through its belly. Hanging on a low Joshua tree branch I almost walked into. Its sleepy lizard eyes were just starting to crust; flies buzzed.

Who would do that? I asked.

A shrike, probably, he said. Or a hawk. Saving it for dinner.

I thought the desert was so peaceful, I said.

No, the desert is so honest, he said.

He saw a bit of trash nearby, a dirty paper flap. He picked it up and tossed it along with my granola bar wrapper into the forest-green Hefty bag in the bed of the truck. He'd brought along a whole collection of plastic bags, from tiny ziplock to body-bag size. *Leave no trace.*

I screamed at the stab to my leg. Josh always camped with his students at official sites with tables and fire grates, but he'd wanted the two of us out in the middle of nowhere. And there we were, only us and the desert and a sere, planeless sky. We'd parked the truck and put on our French Foreign Legion caps and hiked hot silent miles into the wild brush from the road, as requested by park rules for "wilderness camps." The Joshua trees had thinned out as we went farther east. We'd passed rock formations that looked like animals and gourds and human skulls, hiked across bajadas and around granite outcrops. Josh pointed out iguana, skulking coyote, rabbits, squirrels. Desert dandelions and mallow, flame-tipped ocotillo, beavertail, prickly pear. He was walking ahead of me, pushing water and supplies in the small wheelbarrow; he'd told me to walk behind, to obliterate the wheel's track.

Tire marks can live out here for years, he'd said. And they don't belong here. Scars in the desert heal slowly.

Thank you, teacher, I said. But my footsteps don't belong here, either. Don't footsteps count as scars?

We wove our way through creosote bushes and gray-green cactus scrub, breathing hostile air that heated, dusted, and dried my lungs, when I felt my leg seized by sudden hot pierces in the flesh of my right calf, just above my boot. I shrieked. A cylindrical piece of gray-green cactus half a foot long clung to my leg as if Velcro'd, its spines lodged in my skin.

Josh dropped the wagon and ran to me, grabbed my hand before I could reach down.

Uh uh, he said. Don't touch.

Out of nowhere, I said. This thing attacked me out of nowhere. I bit my lip, determined not to cry, split open, fall apart.

Jumping cholla. They're everywhere.

He pointed to a shrubby, fuzzy cactus nearby, three or four feet high, pale green and flowerless. It looked like a bristled balloon animal, twisted from those long, skinny balloons into joints, and covered with spiky hair. It looked mocking.

You must've brushed against it, he said. You step too close to one of those joints, they sense the moisture or heat or energy or something and attack. They jump and cling on.

This is like getting all your childhood vaccinations at once, I said. I wasn't crying, yet.

I told you to be careful.

You told me to be *patient*.

Same thing, he said. He rummaged in his duffel bag. They also call it teddy bear cholla.

Adorable, I said. I pulled the bottle from my backpack and gulped water.

Or silver cholla. They have these silver sheaths on their spines. Look at it, see the sunlight through the spines? See how it shimmers? They're sort of luminous, huh? Pretty?

Josh.

That's good, keep drinking your water. You're breaking out in a sweat. And breathe, Holly.

He came to me with a comb and a pair of pliers. He helped me sit down and propped my leg up on his thighs.

A lot of people think chollas are sort of ugly, he said. Stiff. Stunted-looking. I think they're sort of cool. They get little violet flowers around this time of year. And they're edible, you know? They taste great, sweet, you just have to peel them and—

Josh, do something.

Yeah, hold on.

He slid the comb between my leg and the cactus, threading its teeth among the spines. I swallowed a long drink of water so I wouldn't scream again, maybe my two gallons' worth.

These're called glochids. These little spines, see? They're barbed. They lock in under the top layer of skin. That's how this thing reproduces. The joints cling to whatever passes by. Whatever'll carry it around. Then it lands somewhere and takes root. Chollas are tough. Ranchers hate them; they're like weeds. But medicine men used cholla on people during prayer ceremonies. They believed the spines drew out the sickness.

Josh.

Okay, hold on.

He gripped the comb, then flipped the cactus joint off and away from me, leaving a dozen golden needles still imbedded in my leg, and despite myself, I shrieked again.

Why didn't you warn me? I asked.

I'm sorry.

No, about the cactus. If they're so dangerous.

Okay. I'm warning you now. This is going to hurt. Take a few deep breaths. Try to relax.

One by one he pulled the spines out with pliers. My leg bristled and I shivered at the fierce, tiny burns. I chewed my tongue and swallowed blood while he tried to distract me by teaching me all about cacti. Their survival strategies. How their spines evolved from leaves as a defense against predators, how the reduced leaf surface helped them endure the desert. How their thick, waxy skins retard evaporation, how they're misers, hoarding water in their fleshy stems, in their ribs or barrels or pads of tissue, how during and after a rain they gorge on water, expand and swell to hold as much as they can, how their root systems are shallow but extensive, spreading out wide under a thin surface of dirt to pick up and store moisture from the lightest desert shower. He talked in a smoothing, soothing voice while pulling out the spines. Each spine barb tugged with it a small divot of flesh, a brief welling of blood, and with each tug I thought *Why didn't he warn me? Why did he bring me here, drag me out in the middle of vast nowhere, if this was just going to hurt?* He was trying to get me to relax and succumb to all the landscape and space, to feeling, to feeling small and not clinging to anything, to letting go. As if that weren't dangerous, as if there's any peace in that.

Cacti are actually related to the rose family, did you know that? he was asking. You can see it when they bloom. They blow roses away. Sometimes you can actually watch a cactus flower unfold, the petals open up and uncurl. Actually, they're more beautiful than roses. You expect a rose to be beautiful. It's more interesting to find all that beauty in a cactus. The split personality, you know?

I didn't say anything. I was too angry, I didn't trust myself to speak. Or breathe, I didn't trust the only air there.

Okay, he said. Your spines are gone.

He squeezed my calf hard to bring out the last of the blood, blotted it away with a piece of gauze, then applied antiseptic ointment from the first aid kit. I wiped the sweat off my upper lip. My T-shirt, one of Josh's, was sticking all over; I was sweating too much and too fast for the air to burn it off my skin.

Are you okay? he asked me. He leaned over and pressed his mouth against my damp forehead.

I'm okay, I said.

Drink more water, he mumbled against my hair. I want you guzzling, like, two gallons a day. You need to replace all those fluids.

I nodded, just a small dip of a nod so he wouldn't move his mouth. But he did. He wrapped more gauze in a bandage around my leg, then carefully disposed of the bloodstained gauze in the Hefty garbage bag.

I WASN'T GOING to make love that night. My leg still throbbed, I felt filmed with sweat and sunblock, I wanted to punish Josh for not taking better care of me. We'd zipped our two mummy bags together and I crawled inside with him, determined to stay separate and stiff as wood. But he named the stars for me, and I pressed against him for a sense of scale. He wove his legs between mine so my bandaged calf would rest on top, and I bent my other leg to help. He raised his hand up to trace the constellations, but the parallax distorted their forms; I reached up with him to clasp his hand, trace the sky with him and share his view, horizon, galaxy. He kissed me and then I could breathe again, fully, breathe in the air that was him, breathe in the having him to hold on to, what always made me feel found and unbound, blessed. His touch always split me open into something tender and sweet. He saw in me something luminous, ready to bloom. But it was all him, and he never realized that. I didn't deserve such significance. I didn't deserve him. An elemental, pure, and infinite him, a man who saw the life in a dead lizard, who saw more beauty in a cactus than a rose, who could find the pulse in a petrified limb. A man who didn't realize that I was just a mere me, and that I lived on, drank from, him. And that without him forever as wellspring, as font, I would shrivel up to a small, withered, petty thing and die.

A CACTUS, I said the next morning. I want my very own.

Come on, you *have* your very own. He stopped rolling up our mummy bags to strike an iconic cactus pose.

That's a saguaro, I told him, remembering from *Common Cacti of the Southwest.* They only live in Arizona.

Hey, good.

At the saguaro festival in July they make cactus wine, I told him. It symbolizes rain replenishing the earth.

I'm very proud of you.

And you're a lovely cactus, I said, but this way if you ever leave me, I will always have the real thing. See? I pointed to a small Joshua tree in the distance, an isolated straggler. I waited for him to ask *Why do you think I would ever leave you?*, but he did not.

Ah, he said, smiling his teacher's smile. It said *You are about to learn something,* and I was sick of it. But a Joshua tree is not a cactus. It's a yucca. It's actually part of the lily family.

All right.

Not every desert plant is a cactus, he said. There's yucca and agave and bear grass and ocotillo and creosote and—

All *right!*

He pointed to the ugly killer cholla that had attacked me. *That's* a cactus. Chollas are cacti.

Fine. I'll make do with a cholla. A lowly, ugly, common desert weed.

No.

You thought they were beautiful, I said.

We're not taking a cactus home, he said.

Why not?

He pointed out that the cactus had already wounded me, that I was still complaining about my throbbing leg, and that getting it home would be impossible.

You're scared of a few glochids? I asked. Embrace what you fear.

He sighed. I waited. I waited for him to tell me we can't disrupt the ecosystem of the desert. That tough as cacti are, they're also vulnerable, that we might get it all the way home just to have it refuse to take root and then die. I waited for him to talk about indigenous nutrients in the desert soil, about fungal spores and etiolation. That we didn't have room for the cactus at home, or space for its root system, that the concrete would snuff it out, choke it dead.

This is a national park, he said finally. Everything is protected here.

I wasn't, I said.

We just looked at each other. Then he came and knelt next to me. He put his hand on the back of my skull, wove his fingers through my hair and tugged my head back, put his arms around me. He wanted me to clasp him back, I knew, but I wouldn't give him that. We just sat there for a moment in silence, a heated, taut desert silence. I waited. He gave up first. He got up, took a bottle of water, and hiked all the way back to the truck for the shovel, twine, gloves, a tarpaulin, returned, and dug. I kept watch. We roped the cholla, steadied it in the wheelbarrow, strapped it to the bed of the truck with twine, camouflaged it with Hefty garbage bags, and drove home without talk. We planted the cactus in our found-rock-garden front yard. A week later I found a chipped ceramic Mexican child sleeping beneath its huge ceramic sombrero near a dumpster in the Fairfax District and brought it home. I tried to get Josh to debate whether the ceramic child was racist kitsch or just kitsch, but he only rolled his eyes at me. In the end we put it next to the cactus, facing the street. I called him our little ceramic son. And, as a little ceramic child, it had no moisture or heat or energy, so I knew it would always be safe from the cactus spines and could sleep in peace.

My leg healed, of course. The wound became a spray of small roseate scars. And the cactus did take root in our found-rock plot, did just fine. For two more months it lived and breathed and grew, did very well. I hoped it would blossom soon, give us showy violet flowers. It didn't, but I smiled at it every time I came and went, every time I looked out the window. I admired how the sun on its silvery spines made it shimmer, made it luminous. And every time I thought with pleasure that stealing the cactus was the type of unwholesome, dishonest thing Josh would never have done in front of the junior high and high school kids, or by himself. But I got him to do it for me. I got him to break into the desert for me, plunder it to bring me jewels. I got him to tear a piece off the vastness, chain it down to a bound and finite space. Looking at the cactus always made me feel victorious. I would look at my healed leg scars and think *I am inoculated now, I'm safe.* I felt very peaceful and secure, until two months later, when Josh left me.

JOSH WAS KILLED in a plane crash. Not the kind where you're on the plane. The kind where you start a fight with your girlfriend who loves you to death but who you say won't let you breathe, is too clingy, so you decide to go off hiking by yourself because you need the space, you don't want to do every single thing together, all the time, take and share every single breath with the woman who loves you to death, so you drive out to the Mojave by yourself in your truck, park it, and trek across the desert like Moses, through a field of Joshua trees with their grotesque, outstretched-to-God arms, to sleep under the stars and feel profoundly, vastly insignificant, and far overhead a Cessna Skyhawk SP with engine trouble sails downward, into the welcoming arms, and doesn't see you because you're a mere dot in the landscape, and you don't see it, you just barely awake at the sputter, the swooping whine of what perhaps sounds like a very large desert bird, a hawk, or a screeching owl, or maybe the death cry of a lizard pierced by spikes, and so just as the plane crashes down—*then* you see it, yes, but it's too late—and lands on top of you in a blaze of oil and shredding metal and burning yucca, creosote, ocotillo, maybe your last thought is *I should have kissed the woman I love good-bye when I left*, or *I should have never left her to go outside where it's harsh, unforgiving, dangerous*, or *at least I should have brought her with me so we could die together*. That kind of plane crash. When they dug him out of the cratered brush and found his driver's license, unsinged but the laminate melted into his thigh, they called and told me, and my first thought was *It's not fair to die in a plane crash if you're not actually on the plane*. Then I realized I was shaking and couldn't walk properly, so I crawled into the bathtub. The porcelain was cold, wonderfully solid, anesthetic, and I could pull the shower curtain around to make myself a terrarium. I figured I could sleep there, bathe there, have a water source, have someone bring me packages of ramen to make, I could even shit and pee right there forever, a perfect ecosystem, for the rest of my life, and not ever have to go anywhere or outside again. That worked just fine for three or four days, except for the ramen because I didn't have any, so I just drank a lot of water from the faucet instead, and then Josh's younger brother Paul drove down from Santa Barbara, banged on the front door for a while, then decided to break through the bathroom window to come get me.

He made me get out of the terrarium-tub, and then he decided to stay the night, just to make sure I was okay. He was a sophomore at UC Santa Barbara, studying biology or pre-med or something. Josh had shown me photos of his brother. Paul was seven or eight years younger and unripe-looking, a laundered sweatshirt and ironed jeans, a Josh's kind of hair but combed and darker, a Josh's face but paler, unvarnished. He looked just like the photos, but now he also looked scared, stunned. He got me towels and one of Josh's clean T-shirts and made me take a shower, which seemed ridiculous, given that I'd been living in a bathtub for four days, but fine. When I came out he told me not to worry about anything, that everything had been taken care of, their parents had had Josh's body brought home to Ventura. They'd wanted to find me, have me come for the service, but I'd never answered the phone. They'd always liked me. They thought I was a stabilizing influence on their wandering son. That I could root him. Now they were worried that I was all right. So after the service, because there wasn't time before, Paul had driven down to check. He could stay a few days, he said, then drive back up. I said okay. He'd found sheets and a pillow for the couch. He asked me if I wanted to go out for pizza or something. I looked outside the living room window, at the ugly, treacherous, stolen cholla cactus in the front yard. It had beaten me, gotten me back. I'd stolen Josh, too, and the cactus had punished me for both of them. No, I told Paul, I really didn't feel like going out.

I climbed into bed. Since Josh had left I'd slept far to one side, almost on the edge, so as not to disturb his blanket and mattress space. So his imprint was still there, and a strand of hair, the smell of rock. I thought of his body burned into the California desert, if the heat had turned the desert sand to glass. I wondered how long the scar of his footsteps' trek would last. I wondered if they searched for and found every last shred of him, packed up every scrap in tiny ziplock bags. *Leave no trace.* Or if a limb was left behind. A dead, rotting Josh limb, now food and home for the termites and kangaroo rats, his energy recycled, transformed. He would have liked that.

I got up and went back to sleep in the bathtub.

AFTER A FEW weeks, Paul had the idea to transfer to UCLA. He decided to just forget about fall quarter at UCSB so he could stay in L.A. and hang out with me, then start winter quarter down here. What he *really* wanted to do, he confided one night, was drop out altogether and do something really cool and free-spirited like Josh. He didn't *really* want to be a doctor, but his parents were pretty invested in it. In one of their sons achieving, being successful. And *now*, you know. . . . His voice trailed off. He asked me if I had talked to my parents. If maybe I wanted him to call them for me. And I said No, they never even met Josh, I haven't even seen them for a few years. We've never been very close. They're not your kind of parents, all nurturing and invested, I told him. My parents were always off being very busy, always leaving me to go off by themselves.

Paul was sleeping in the bed by then. I'd given him Josh's space. I was sleeping in the bathtub, but I'd leave the door ajar and the shower curtain tugged open to talk at night until we fell asleep. And after a few months he decided he didn't *really* need to get his own apartment, that he should probably stay with me so I wouldn't be all alone and he could take care of me. I gave him Josh's clothing to wear, all of which is too big for him and full of threadbare spots, but he likes it. He wears Josh's French Foreign Legion caps. Josh would have liked that, too. Their parents call every few weeks to see how we're doing. I hear Paul tell them he's worried about me. They tell Paul they read an article that says the first year is the hardest, but then it gets better. They tell Paul they're going to send the article, so that I can read it. They say they want to come visit us. None of them seems to realize it's my fault we all lost him. That it's because of me we all have to cling to each other and shrivel up and pay.

Paul tries so hard. He goes to the grocery store and makes us pizza from scratch. He goes to the laundromat. He downloads all of the newest releases, because I won't even debate the idea of going out. He seems to think I'm very fragile, about to wilt and expire, or explode. He says he doesn't like to leave me alone, but I think he just doesn't like to go out by himself. I urge him to go.

I tell him *We don't have to spend all of our time together, do we?* I tell him to make some friends from school. I tell him he needs to give me more space, and his scared look has started coming back.

I'M ASLEEP THE night he comes home sometime in April, after hanging out with his new friends from school. I wake up because he's loud and stumbling, a little drunk, and comes into the bathroom to tug on my arm. *Please, Holly,* he says, *wake up. Please come sleep in the bed with me tonight.* He strokes my hair and my shoulder. We've never touched. We've been together almost a year, and we've never even slightly brushed against each other. I barely even sense him in the apartment, rarely sense his energy or heat. He starts crying now, *I miss Josh,* he says, trying to grip me, *I'm lonely, please, isn't it time, aren't you lonely?* and I think *What difference does it make?* I let him pull me out of the tub's cool hug and pull me into the bedroom. We get in the bed together, both of us in Josh's T-shirts, and he's fondling, clutching at me. My skin just feels numb. It's dead skin, and he's rubbing me as if trying to make it alive. He enters me, I'm dry as dust and I don't even feel it. He's trying to get further inside me, and I realize, then, what he's really trying to do. Get me to unfold, to pulse. It's April, and he's trying to get me to flower again. He's trying to peel back a layer of me to get where it's pulpy and soft. He's feeling so much, and he's trying to make me feel, too, expose me to where it's dangerous and full of unseen, searing threat. He's touching me as if he's capable of that. But he isn't. He's weak, insignificant, a pale imitation. And he's just clutching at me because I'm here, not because I mean anything, am anything to him, really, he's just clinging to whatever happened by. Anyway, I won't let it happen. I suddenly see myself making love to Josh, then, opening up to all of it, I feel myself start to get wet and I chew my tongue to bleed and keep me from it, so I won't cry, fall apart, split open into the tenderness and the sweet. I hold myself stiff as wood, I gulp and gulp to hoard up all the wet, keep it inside of me, and when he finally finishes I gasp and prickle with relief.

I LIKE TO keep the front door triple-locked, and it takes me a moment to remember, deadbolt first, that's right, then knob. I leave the chain on and peek out through the gap at the empty street, the sleeping ceramic child, the cactus. It's grown bigger. It's taller than I am now, cuddly and blameless-looking, its spines silver and luminous in the moonlight. I unchain the front door and step outside. The outside air feels exactly the same as the inside air, and I think *Of course, there is no difference.* It isn't safe anywhere you go.

The cactus is waiting for me, and very welcoming. It isn't punishing or mocking; it's kind. It knows I want my spines back.

It knows my moisture, heat, energy, and yearns toward me. It yearns toward my legs, first, my thighs, then the insides of my open arms, my throat, embraces me even before I've pressed against it with my breasts, attaches to every inch of my skin with its greedy tines. The cactus needs me. It finds me significant, and I embrace it back, hard, to feel its spines enter and become mine. Each pierce creates a vivid bloom. Each spine taps my blood, then my bones, and this makes me feel boundless, and vast. And this is something I can succumb to, this is something I can feel.

BALL

My sweet little dog, Tess, is what they call "apricot." She has tiny blue eyes, almond-shaped and set close together like Barbra Streisand's, and the prettiest little dog vagina. I spent twenty minutes examining and marveling at it once with my best friend, Dayna, before she had a boyfriend and we spent a lot of our time together appreciating Tess. Dayna is a biologist, which gave the experience a legitimizingly clinical spirit. It's a tidy, quarter-inch slit in a pinky-tip protuberance of skin, delicate and irrelevant and veiled with fine, apricot hair. Tess rolled over and spread out happily, trustingly, for us; she lives almost pathetically for love, for attention, like a quivering heroine from some '50s romance novel. She also lives for food and naps, but mostly for Ball. Tennis balls, squishy rubber ones with bells inside, any spherical object to love will do. I've learned hard rubber balls are the best—the last time she had a flimsy plastic one she worked it down to bits, chewed it with such passion there was almost nothing left.

She came with a ball. I'd been living alone in my big new house with a fireplace for six days, came home on a Thursday evening to the still-lingering smell of paint and spackle and fresh-sliced carpet fibers and realized *I can have a dog here.* Apartment living hadn't allowed for that, but now I had my own house with a fireplace and a small fiberglass jacuzzi in a small chlorine-scented backyard, all to myself. I was only twenty-five and very proud of having my own house. I walked around and around, and my heels clacked resoundingly on the hardwood floors. Dayna had mentioned maybe coming over, but we'd hung out together the last five nights out of six, she was in a needy, boyfriend-less phase, and her presence was becoming a cloying and oppressive force. She hated sleeping alone—she's always scared of an earthquake, a fire combusting out of nowhere, a serial-killer-rapist-burglar breaking in—but I wanted my big, new house all to myself, and a dog, and a fire in the fireplace. I went right back out and bought a newspaper and called the first ad for a cockapoo: *eleven mos, shots, fxd, hsbrkn, plyful.* A cockapoo, to me, meant the large dark eyes of a baby harp seal and a silky spaniel coat, a body thick-limbed but compact and floppy. The true, Platonic image of a cockapoo. I drove to an apartment complex in Northridge. The dog was hideous, at first sight, more blurred, cross-bred terrier and toy poodle than anything else, with skinny, crooked legs that needed to be broken and reset, and those creepy blue eyes. A brown nose, faded like over-creamed coffee. And she was covered with fleas, little dark leaping specks visible through her beige fur. I made polite chat with the owner, a heavy sixtyish black woman named Gloria—*That isn't beige, dear, they call that color "apricot" on a poodle*—who couldn't be bothered with the dog anymore, and then told her that Yes, I knew the ad *said* she'd be eleven months, but I really did want a puppy. The dog dropped a soiled, shreddy, lime-colored tennis ball in front of me and looked up, her tiny eyes squinting with hope and expectation: *You want to play with my ball? Here, look, here's a ball! You want to play? Please, please!* When I ignored her she pounced on the ball with her skinny front legs, her paws shoving it toward me— *Ball! Ball! Ball!*—until I gave in and threw it for her. But when I got up to leave, I suddenly realized that if I didn't take her, it meant I would have to keep interviewing dogs. This seemed like an exhausting prospect: continuing to call deceptive ads, inquire about worms, meet imperfect dogs, choose. Also, it meant that I would be going home that night to my big house alone. I told Gloria I would take the dog, figuring that if it didn't work out I would just get rid of it somehow. I wrote Gloria a check for seventy-five dollars—the cost of getting the dog fixed at five months, and the shots—and she gave me a leash, a quarter of a bag of Puppy Chow, and the dog. At the last moment, Gloria put the soiled tennis ball in the Puppy Chow bag, like a parting gift. *The dog's gotta have that ball*, she said, *or any kind of ball, you'll see.* I stopped at the drugstore on the way home with the dog, to buy flea shampoo and dog treats, and I dumped the dirty, lime-hairy ball in a dumpster. Through the window of the car the dog watched me do this, anxious, her squinty little eyes made wide and round by alarm.

At home she suffered submissively, mournfully, through the kitchen-sink flea bath and a towel-drying in front of a fire in the fireplace, then curled up tight as a snail shell at the foot of my bed, looking orphaned and weepy. She wouldn't touch the doggy rag tug thing I'd bought, nor the faux-bone treats, nor the plastic squeaky toy shaped like a garish hamburger with the works. I went to bed wondering how to unload an ugly and sentient animal. Several hours later I heard a light *thud* sound, then a *thump-roll, thump-roll,* and I looked across my room to see the little dog trotting happily toward the bed with a Granny Smith apple in her mouth. She jumped up on the bed with it, dropped it, peered up squintily with hope and expectation, and shoved it toward me with her crooked apricot paws. I knew I'd bought apples during the week, but how she'd found one I had no idea—some desperate, biologically driven search for Ball. I threw the apple across the room for her for a while, and each time she brought it back to me, thrilled, suffused with intimate joy at our connection. She finally tired, snail-curled on the empty pillow next to me, and went to sleep. When I awoke in the morning her brown nose was breathing in my face and her almond-shaped blue eyes blinked at me with drowsy adoration, and I was abruptly slapped swollen with love. I went out first thing and bought her a real ball, periwinkle blue, hard rubber, just the right size and with a solid, stable bounce.

Now it isn't just my echoing footsteps in the house, it's her happy, scratchy nail-scrambles, the thud and roll of a ball that I hear.

I loved her so much it was numbing, and sometimes, to jab a feeling at myself, I fantasized about her dying. Getting hit by a car, drinking from a contaminated puddle of water when we went on walks (how my accountant Sue's dog died), or succumbing to an attack of bloat (some disease my friend Lesley's dog almost died of, when the intestines bunch up out of nowhere). Or I would whet the fantasy by imagining that I had to sacrifice her for some reason. Put her out of some misery. I'd have her dying of encroaching cancers, where I forced myself to give her a mercifully quick and lethal shot of morphine because keeping her alive and in pain would only fulfill my own selfish needs. This usually made me cry, and once, picturing that and crying, I called Dayna and made her promise me if Tess ever did get sick she'd get drugs and a syringe from the lab, and we'd take care of it so Tess would never suffer. Or I'd think about an epic disaster, a nuclear bomb or a 9-point earthquake that somehow destroyed all the food and left me with nothing but Tess, and would I be willing to starve to death instead of eat her. How bad something would have to get to force me to do such a thing. I wondered what Tess would taste like. I imagined her flesh was tender and sweet. Her paw pads were the color of cracked, grayish charcoal and smelled of burned popcorn. When she yawned I poked my nose into the gap of her jaw and inhaled. I ran my hands over the wiry pubic-like hairs at the base of her spine, the fine, clumped curls at her throat. She let her head fall all the way back when I did this, so trusting, her throat stretched to a soft, defenseless, apricot sweep. I just wanted to crawl inside of her sometimes, or have her crawl inside of me, keep her safe there forever.

In hindsight, Gloria's ad was accurate; Tess was indeed *fxd*—you could still feel the barbed wire of subcutaneous stitches in her belly, another thing Dayna and I always marveled at, or used to, before Dayna met her boyfriend, back when hanging out meant admiring and playing Ball with Tess for hours at a time—and *hsbrkn*, and I was spared all the yipping, newspaper-thwacking, stick-her-nose-in-it hassles of a puppy. The idea of disciplining her horrified me, and I was glad I didn't have to. Her one unfortunate habit was her way of hurtling herself at people to greet them when they came in the door, invariably impacting at ovarian- or testicular-crushing height. Dayna encouraged this, finding the hurtling a consistent and unconditional show

of love; she'd catch Tess in mid-leap, grab her at each side's delicate, curving haunch, and swoop her around the living room
or the backyard like a clumsy, older puppy-sister. Tess's exu-
berance, her insistence on playing Ball, worked as sort of a
litmus test for other people—how much grace they mustered
up told me a lot about who they were. But most people adored
her. Some friends perfected a knee-dip-and-swivel, so that Tess
landed smack against a fleshy mid-thigh. Eric showed a conge-
nial grace about it the first time he came over to my house, but
after that it became his means to set the evening's tone; if he
was feeling generous he petted her, threw the ball for her, and
we had a stressless, fun, prurient kind of time together, but if
he wasn't in the mood or thought I was paying too much attention to her, he got nasty. Sometimes there was a faintly sinister quality to it, especially when she wanted to play Ball and
he didn't. Sometimes it became an enraging, bitter thing. He'd
hide the ball, laughing as she searched the house in a growing
panic. Or he'd pretend to throw it but then hide it behind his
back and smirk at her bewilderment. If she shoved the ball at
him once too often—and she could be relentless, needy, *You
want to play with my ball? Here, look, here's a ball! You want to
play? Please, please!*—his annoyance built to the point where I
got very nervous and protective, almost scared he was going to
explode and hurt her. I'd try to distract him with food or sex.
Sometimes I think he hated her, but then he'd be so sweet and

loving I'd figure it would all be okay. He liked coming to my place because of the fireplace and the jacuzzi, but it still usually felt safer to me if I just went alone to his.

I MET ERIC two years ago, when Dayna had a big party to celebrate getting a promotion at her lab, something that involved a bonus and increased time with rabbits. She told me she'd invited a couple of young guys who'd moved in across the street; one of them had a girlfriend but the other was exactly my type, and also the type who probably wouldn't go for her, anyway. Dayna is very beautiful, she just has a way of thrusting herself at men, emotionally stripping for them on a first date. She assumes men prefer me because I'm smaller—she's six feet tall, stunning, but six feet tall—while I think it's just because she tries too hard, opens up too massively. She drowns you with all of herself, with a flood of vulnerability, trust, need, and I know that the success of sex depends on contrivance, in holding yourself back. It's the tease, not the strip. You offer up your soul for a taste; it's like an invitation to feed.

Eric turned out to be twenty-three, six years younger than Dayna and me, and striking, a wonderfully alpine six feet four, which was certainly tall enough for Dayna, but I saw what she meant by my type—tall and bold men always make me feel sexual, nymphetish—and also what she meant by he probably wouldn't go for her, anyway. He didn't want a drowning torrent of intimacy; he wanted to get laid. We sat on the floor of Dayna's apartment for an hour at the party's wane, drinking beer and making suggestive, clever comments to each other while he played Ball with Tess. He petted her and scratched her tummy, not realizing that being sweet to my sweet little dog was a litmus test of sexual acceptability, a wildly effective and endearing form of foreplay. She adored him, draped herself trustingly across his lap, her little almond eyes slanted closed in bliss. But that wasn't why I wanted him, badly, really; it was the adamant and unabashed sex look of him, his way of dirty, lustful regard. His look said *Sex*, said *Fuck, suck me, I'm hard*, said *It's specifically, singularly, because of you*. I suddenly realized I hadn't been fully looked at that way in a while, maybe a long while. It used to happen all the time, but not so often anymore. Eric looked at me that way, and I wanted to get his cock inside me, fast, to hold on to that look. His hands stroking Tess's tummy—I wanted them on me, working me, shoving my thighs apart, pressing me face down by my shoulders or the back of my neck into a pillow, raising my hips high from behind, guiding my head. I wanted to leave with him that second, but I knew Dayna would be upset. So I waited another half hour to suggest he show me his new place across the street, and in answer he circled me hard around the waist, leaned over, and kissed me—more gently than I'd expected, but still his arm was firm, ruling—and then we left. I took Tess with me, and her latest in the series of hard rubber periwinkle blue balls; Dayna had wanted us to sleep over, but hey, she was the one who'd tossed me this guy in the first place.

I hate fucking men who get moony or coy about it, who act as if there's an element of accident that you're here, doing this, as if you both tripped and wound up landing naked in bed. Eric was brusque and unsheepish, as fearless of sex as a porn star. He had the hard, tapered male torso I like, skin so fluid and seamless your hand slides, slides. My own skin is starting to dry, slightly— I shouldn't go in the jacuzzi too often—I've noticed fine, thin wrinkles when I twist the loosening flesh of my upper arms, I've grown a little self-conscious of my babyish pout of belly. But the sex was an endlessly wet, vehement, pounded smooth kind of sex that wiped out doubt.

During the first surge of it, on Eric's living room sofa—a velour playpen-style couch still smelling faintly of frat house joints and beer—Tess had stretched out drowsily at the far end, behind Eric's hunching, jarring back, out of his view. We reeled to his bed afterward, while he was still solid and driven and I could still jolt at a slightest touch of his tongue, to start all over. She picked up her ball and padded after us, climbed upon a bolster we'd thrown on the floor, and went back to sleep. I'd had Tess for a little over four years by then but had never fucked anyone with her in the room before; I typically went to the guy's house and left afterward, because, after all, Tess would be home, waiting for me, needing to go out. I liked my bed all to ourselves. After the second time, I got up, awkwardly—my legs felt permanently locked apart at the hips, hinged wide—and fumbled for clothing, but Eric grabbed an ankle and pulled me back onto the quilted bedspread. Mock-wrestle, mock-struggle, and Tess jumped up on the bed with us to play, her mouth full of periwinkle ball. He had me pinned on my side, was fumbling with himself, aiming, when Tess dropped and shoved her ball at him—*Get out of here, dog, go on*, he said—wedging it under his thigh—*You want to play with my ball? Here, look, here's a ball! You want to play? Please, please!*— and kept shoving, desperate for his attention, his affirming and engaged throw of the ball. I tried squirming upward, trying to glide, grasp him inside me, distract him, but one more ball-shove from Tess—*Would you get her the fuck out of here?* he snapped at me—and he jerked out a leg, catching her just at her midsection's arching curve, and hurled her off the bed. She yelped, I saw in the streetlamp's light through the window an apricot blur, and heard her smack the wall, heard her flurry slide to the ground.

I was up and to her in a second—*Hey, I'm sorry, I didn't mean to do that, okay?*—and she was fine, just bewildered. She poked her damp pink tongue in my ear and hiccupped like a little human baby, and I cradled her, rubbing her tummy. She was fine, but I wanted to cry. Eric kept apologizing, coaxing me back, and when I looked at him in disgust he finally said I was overreacting, just being neurotic, I shouldn't indulge her so much, I was probably going to wind up some weird old lady living alone with forty-seven poodles. I carried her out of the bedroom, slamming the door behind us. Then I didn't know what to do. It was almost three, I knew Dayna was asleep, and I didn't want to go wake her up, explain what had happened. She'd be furious; worse, she'd be smug. And Tess's ball was still in the bedroom with Eric; I wasn't leaving without it. I wasn't going to leave her without a ball.

I carried her into Eric's roommate's bedroom—he was staying at his girlfriend's, Eric had told me—and crawled with her into the unmade bed, into unwashed sheets with that odor of careless, straight, young bachelor guys. She dozed on the greasy pillow next to me, in her spine-defying, shell-curled way, her nose in my face. I tried to go to sleep. My jaw ached; I scratched away some flakes of dried semen on my cheek, craved a drink of water, but didn't want to get up. My insides still felt stretched open, rooted out. My hips kept twitching in the rhythm I'd found sent him over. I'd already gotten to know the thick vein in bas-relief on the left side of his cock, and the exact, utmost length within me his fingers could go, and I wanted all of that back. I wanted that obliterating lust, heated and direct and unrefracted as rays of light through a magnifying glass, focused to burn you down to death. I heard Tess yawn, and I craned to face her, needing the comforting, starfish scent of her breath.

I waited until she was asleep, then got up, stealthily closed the roommate's door behind me, and crept back into Eric's room. He'd thrown half the bedspread over himself and lay sleeping, sprawled out and mammoth and lustrous. I molded myself small up against the length of him and felt a flutter of pulse down his arm; I crawled on top of him and slid myself around until he grew big and hard and I could grip at that vivid, affirming burn one more time.

In the morning we glanced disdainfully at each other and rolled quickly out of opposite sides of the bed. I retrieved Tess's ball and hurried to free her from the other room; she kissed me wildly, whimpering, as though she'd feared something had happened to me in the night, that I'd left her forever. He watched me nuzzle her for a moment—*I guess that's the deal breaker, huh?* he said—then shrugged and went back into his room. Dayna looked at me like a resigned, just slightly reproachful good loser when I came in, then shrieked a greeting to Tess, whipped her up to a leaping, hurtling frenzy, and swooped around the room with her. We spent the rest of the morning cleaning up the party's dismal mess and playing Ball. Eric called me at home the next day, and I invited him over for the following Saturday night; he came bearing a single iris for me and a bag of pricey lamb-and-rice treats for Tess. He let her climb onto his lap, and she spread herself out happily for him, unguarded, unself-conscious, arching her head and exposing her throat to his fondling, stroking hand. He threw the ball for her that night, again and again. But after that I usually insisted on going to his place and leaving Tess with Dayna, where it was safe.

I WAS CAREFUL never to sleep with him again, even after a year. I didn't want to get slack, or too accessible, and actually sleeping together was hardly the point. The only time I did fall asleep, after that first grotesque night and morning, was just an accident, a slip. Tess was across the street with Dayna, and the plan, as always, was the requisite dinner with Eric while we watched a movie or a rerun of *The Simpsons*, then sex, and then I would leave. I just wanted pizza or Chinese delivered, something quick, because the dinner was not the point either, just a feature he liked to insist on, but I got to his apartment and smelled onions cooking, mushrooms, the acrid snap of garlic. He was making dinner. His roommate was out, and he was making an evening, trying to, out of a Lyle Lovett CD and a head of romaine lettuce and a jar of Ragú sauce spiffed up with fresh onions and mushrooms—*Hey, come on, I really like to cook, my mom told me to add all these veggies*, he said, nodding—and a gleaming bottle of red zinfandel. A boiling pot of spaghetti fogged the kitchen with starch; the table was set with melamine plates and paper towel napkins folded in big squares. Fine, okay. I started on the wine, had half the bottle down by the end of salad, and listened to him talk about some old college girlfriend, some Shannon or Nicole, whom he'd been with for a couple of years and really cared about but just was never ready to commit to and how he'd heard the other day she was getting married and he really did hope she was happy but it still really hurt, you know, and it was probably time he started really thinking about what he was going to do with his life, about what he wanted in life, and what did I think about all that? And what I was thinking was that it was getting late and we'd never had sex yet on his kitchen table and can we get going? And that Tess was waiting for me over at Dayna's and I've finished my spaghetti and can we get going? I tipped the last of the wine into my mouth, got up, slid off my underwear from under my skirt, and he shut up. I sat on his lap, straddling him, pushed his hand down in the crotch of space between us, used my hand against the buttons on his jeans, and his breathing quickened. I traced the rim of his ear with my tongue, worked myself against his fingers, everything I knew would do it, and it did, his cock jutting out from his split-open fly and the table edge gouging my spine when he lunged forward at me. I leaned back with my elbows on the table, skirt raised and legs open, for him to get me up and onto it, but instead he picked me up—*Uh uh, not here*, he mumbled—clutching and carrying me like a sack of fragile groceries, kissing me before we even got to his room. He fell with me on the bed, fell onto me with a great, weighted crush, but when I squirmed to get up on my hands and knees for him he gently pushed me flat again, face down, nudging my legs apart, *Good, I like that*, I said, *do that*, and then twisted my shoulders around so that while he thrust into me from behind, lying on me, he had my face against his, or his face in my neck, still kissing me. That kind of twist was a strain, everything went taut and seized up until it hurt so I couldn't stand it anymore; I finally had to pull back away from him, turn away. I pressed my face down into the pillow but he wouldn't let me do that, wanted my arm around his shoulders or his neck, holding on, wanted me facing him, and twisted me back. It took a long time. He kept slowing down and every time I was about to come he wouldn't let me, he'd just stop, still looking at me, and when we both finally came in the middle of a kiss that was like breathing straight into each other's lungs we stayed like that, still, all twisted up around each other. When my spine and the rest of me finally relaxed, went aimless, all of my muscles eased into place and I strayed off to sleep. Eric still on top of me, holding me. A branch hitting the window lurched me awake well after midnight, and my first aware thought was a glad one, *Thank God that woke me up so I can get out of here.*

I pulled away from Eric and called Dayna—Yeah, Tess was okay, she was right there on the pillow next to her. I told Dayna I was coming over, I'd be there soon. Proof I was a good friend, always there for her, this guy doesn't mean anything to me, see, and she wasn't just a babysitter. Eric tugged on the phone in my hand, *No, come on, don't leave, she's fine,* but I shook my head at him until he let go. He was angry, I could see in the light from the streetlamp through the window, and that pleased me. I could imagine him thinking there was something wrong with me that I'd leave him to go running off to my dog. He rolled over to the other side of the bed, a big, spoiled baby, *Fine, go,* his back to me; I got up and straightened out my clothes and left without saying good-bye. He needed to learn, I thought, that he can't have everything he wants. That he was only there to fuck, I'd never be lulled, and in the end, if he ever pushed me, I would always choose my sweet little dog.

WHEN I WENT to Sausalito, Tess stayed with my mother. An artist friend asked me to house-sit for six weeks while he went to Eastern Europe to study iconography; I decided leaving town would wave a giant *Fuck You* flag at Eric, a banner of my insusceptibility. I decided it was time for a more sporadic arrangement, that it would keep everything fervent and honed. I told my artist friend I'd love to get out of town for a while. The only problem: no dogs. He was wildly allergic. I insisted to him that poodles don't shed, and that Tess was mostly poodle, I thought, but he wasn't about to come home to dander and tracked-in spores. He was apologetic, but that was the deal. I decided it was worth it, that Eric needed to be reminded what this was, and I reminded myself that contrivance works. It does, I'm telling you. Dayna was hurt and upset, as if I were abandoning her. She was also upset she couldn't take Tess—her hours at the lab made it impossible. So I packed up Tess's food and water dishes, her special high-quality food the vet had recommended, her leash, her blue rubber ball, and drove her over to my mom's. I started crying when I hugged Tess good-bye—*Don't worry, honey, she's my grandchild, isn't she? I'll take very, very good care of her*—and she burrowed her face in the crook of my neck. I was a terrible mother, to do this to her, and for what, for *him*? I pushed my nose into her charcoal-colored paw pads to breathe in the salty, furry, puppy-sweat smell, then forced myself to leave. I cried for a few hours afterward, choked with guilt, still seeing her forlorn, confused face as I drove off without her.

NOT WAKING UP to Tess was awful. I walked through Sausalito two or three times a day—gift shop, gallery, gift shop, gallery, driftwood seagulls everywhere—and when I found people with dogs, I would befriend them. Guys with dogs thought I was coming on to them, but I just wanted the dogs. One Sunday I met a retired policeman from Oakland, walking a docile, regal borzoi. This was an odd dog for a policeman to have, a guy with a movie cop's burly swagger and black kangaroo-leather shoes. Long before Tess, I'd thought of having a borzoi one day; they're hugely magnificent Art Deco dogs with dear, shy temperaments, but they're also congenitally stupid. This one was skittish, too, and pulled nervously from my greeting—the guy told me she'd been part of a case he'd investigated, that she'd been abused and abandoned by some volatile, coked-up perp, and afterward he'd adopted her. Cynthia. He said abused dogs broke his heart, even more than abused kids, because dogs are even more vulnerable and trusting, their lives are in our hands and they know it. And they *are* like kids; they even love the people who abuse them, you know? There's that innate instinct to adapt, adjust. He'd like to see animal abuse laws toughened up. Cynthia was his baby now, *Yeah, my precious little girl, Daddy's always gonna take good, fine care of you, uh huh.* She bumped her long muzzle into his stomach, leaned against him so fully and hard he almost lost his balance. She trusted me to pet her for a while then, and I ran my fingers through her long, sheening white coat, wishing for Tess. The guy looked like he maybe wanted to keep talking, or go for coffee, but I just wanted to pet Cynthia. Yeah, I told him, because animals had purer souls than human beings—everybody has his own agenda and wants something from you, even friends, even lovers, even your mother, and you can't let your guard down, ever, that's when they get you, hurt you—and so animals were more honest, more deserving of love and care. I told him I had a little apricot cockapoo I just loved to death, who was everything pure and innocent and sweet in the world, whom I'd do anything for, and the idea of actually getting married and having actual children was revolting to me, because you couldn't fully ever trust a human being, a friend, a parent, a lover, they love you, they hurt you, you can't even trust yourself, whereas a dog like Tess would be there for you, always. I told him I shouldn't even be away from her here in Sausalito, I should hurry home, because I was just wasting six weeks of her life—she wasn't a puppy anymore, she was a grown-up dog, and I'd sacrificed six precious weeks of her life away from her, just to be here alone, a big, gaping crater of a person with nothing to hold inside. I told him I felt I could never get close enough to her, keep her safe enough from harm, because I wasn't really worthy of her, and because the world and everyone in it was so profoundly fucked. I asked him if he wanted to go get coffee or a drink or something, but he tugged a little on Cynthia's leash, and said it was nice meeting me, but they had to get going.

MY MOTHER ALWAYS apologized on the phone that she couldn't possibly give Tess the kind of attention I gave her—she just couldn't play Ball all the time, it was too much. It was like having a child in the house again, Like when *you* were little, honey, she'd say, Always wanting attention, so *needy*, a person could go nuts from it, from the constant demand, a person can't help losing her patience. A person can't help losing it, now and then. Sometimes something just *snaps*, she would say, her voice a remembered echo, a long-lost refrain. And you can't give in to giving them love all the time, the real world's not like that, and they have to learn. If you do, it just spoils a child, they learn how to be manipulative, and Tess, well, she *is* a little spoiled, honey, she *could* use some discipline. And she was acting maybe a little depressed.

I assured my mother that Tess loved being at her house and I knew she was taking very good care of her, doing the best she could, but part of me felt a little nervous and protective. I drove home a week early; I sort of expected to find Tess ragged and thin and hungry, like the orphans at the beginning of *Oliver*, and my mother snapping, clutching the hairbrush, a spatula, a coiled fistful of telephone cord. But Tess was fine, hurtling herself at me in joy, whimpering when I clutched her, quivering with unrestrained love. On the way home in the car she lay down with a happy exhalation and put her head in my lap.

Her ball, however, was on its last gasp. Somehow the hard rubber ball I'd left her when I went to Sausalito had gotten lost, and my mother had bought her a flimsy yellow plastic one with fake, porcupiney spikes. I'd been so clear with my mother about this, very specific about what Tess needed in a ball, but of course she hadn't listened, my mother. I should never have trusted her. The plastic had split under Tess's vehement play, and only an inch or so of its circumference seam held the ball together—it wasn't even really a ball anymore, it was an asymmetrical yellow plastic flap. But for some reason, Tess was madly in love with it. When we got home and I gave it to her, she ran around and around with it, the chewed yellow plastic flapping from either side of her mouth.

I checked my voicemail messages, something I'd airily refrained from doing the entire time I was away. One, from Dayna, of course, welcoming me home. I hadn't called Eric to tell him I was leaving, but Dayna had mentioned to him where I was. I assumed he'd learn I was back, or when I was coming back, in the same way. I'd assumed he'd call, want us to get together. Maybe he'd call later. *Call me, call me, call me*, I chanted to the phone. I dialed his number. His roommate's voice answered, and I hung up. Tess perked her ears and hopefully dropped the plastic flap in front of me, expecting it to roll like a ball. When it wouldn't, she just made do, picked it up again, dropped it closer so I could reach, and shoved it my way. But my spine was petrified from the long drive home, and I decided to go in the jacuzzi; that way, when Eric called, I wouldn't be just sitting there, waiting for him.

The hot water sent up pungent steam; I'd poured in way too much chlorine before leaving for Sausalito, and it was now like boiling myself in disinfectant. It felt good; I let the jets pound on my back. Tess trotted up, dropped the yellow ball-flap at the jacuzzi's lip—*No, honey, not now*, I said—and then shoved it into the bubbling water; it swirled around then flapped closed, trapping in the water's weight, and sank slowly to the bottom. I ignored it, but Tess went wild, whining desperately to have it back. I had to dive under to retrieve it, the heat and the chlorine searing my eyes, then tossed it back to her with a firm admonition—*That's it, Tess, no more Ball, not now*—but she did it again, then again, in that relentless, needy *Ball! Ball! Ball!* way, just when *I* needed something, to relax—*Stop it, just stop it!* I snapped—then again, just to *get* me, I knew it, until finally I came up with it, burning, just in time to hear a phone ring's trill. Or, I thought, listening for it. The jets were loud and I wasn't sure I heard a ring, but then I was sure I did, but then Tess barked at me, crying for the ball I still held, and so then I wasn't sure. But then there was nothing. She began to whine and whine—*All right, you want it, you want the fucking ball?*—and I threw it as far as I could over the backyard fence, probably into a neighbor's yard or garage space. *Go get it, go!* She whimpered pitifully, and I hated her, suddenly, wanted to punish her for all the obsessive, manipulative Ball bullshit, her pathetic, obvious need for love that I'd always given in to and had made me such an idiot, had cost me so much. I shoved her hard away from the edge of the jacuzzi, ready to snap her spine, ready to make it all stop. She just looked at me, bewildered and wounded, and meekly rolled over on her back on the jacuzzi-splashed concrete, her crooked little paws raised in supplication.

The only message on the machine was the old one from Dayna. I hurriedly got dressed, got Tess back in the car—she crept into the backseat this time, burrowed herself down behind my seat like she'd done a horrible, inexcusable thing—and drove over to Dayna's. Eric's car was parked in front of his place, but if he saw me, hey, I was just there to see my friend Dayna. But she had someone over, a guy, some short, rabbity fellow biologist from the lab, who smiled and poured me a glass of wine but kept gazing at her with a moony, indulgent expression. She didn't even marvel at Tess, just let her jump up once or twice, then told her nicely to get down. I waited an hour to ask her if she'd seen or talked to Eric recently, and she mentioned something about their going to the grocery store together a few times, a jog in the park. He'd taken a weekend trip to La Jolla with some buddies, but that was a few weeks ago; he'd told her the trip was great, they'd all gotten laid. And she'd seen him a few times since with some really cute girl, coming or going from his building. She looked at me, smugly, I thought, maybe sort of challengingly. As if I'd tell her anything. As if I'd tell her I pictured him fucking some moist-skinned twenty-two-year-old, spreading her legs and eating her on the velour playpen couch or the kitchen table, telling her *Fuck me,* his look saying *Suck me, I'm hard,* and *It's specifically, singularly, because of you,* and how it made me want to drive nails into both of them, all of them. It was pretty late, and obvious Dayna and her biologist wanted to be alone, so I picked up Tess and we left. I was glad Dayna had found someone, but it seemed just a little sad to me, pathetic, that she'd grabbed at the first guy not smashed flat by the plunging, falling safe of her need.

OUTSIDE TESS STARTED pulling on her leash. As if to get away from me. I apologized, I bent over and tried to rub her tummy, *It was my fault*, I told her, *I was the one who took away your ball, I'm sorry, I just lost it for a minute*, but she wouldn't even look at me. Even if she did, I suddenly knew I'd see hate in her little blue eyes, betrayal, distrust, disgust, and that made me want to bawl, crumple up, just die. Pound her into loving me again. She seemed to want to cross the street, or I thought she did, so I let out the leash a few feet and let her go. She trotted directly across to where the streetlight was in front of Eric's apartment house, the one that always shone through the tree branches into his bedroom window. She sniffed around the grass, squatted and peed, but then still tugged me, really, she did, across the patch of landscaping, toward the dark window at the side of the building. And I looked through the window, knowing what I was going to see, the heat and the wet, the feral rocking, a thing to draw blood, flaming and lethal as love. But all I could see, I thought, was a still, dull gleam of torso, and then a curve, maybe, of breast, a rumple of long dark hair, a girl sleeping curled up inside his arms, the quilted bedspread half thrown over both of them, all of it, both of them, still. I looked over at Tess; she gazed at me with innocence, the light from the streetlamp making a nimbus of her fine apricot fur.

SHE WOULD HAVE been seven on her next birthday, and that's starting to get old, sort of, for a dog. She would have gotten arthritis, or canine diabetes, and I couldn't do that to her. I wouldn't be able to bear seeing her in any pain, or seeing her hurt, and I bet Dayna would be just too busy with her drooly boyfriend when the time came to help. I got a fire going in the fireplace, and I brought her onto my lap and held her for a while. I felt the tiny staple-stitches inside her belly where she'd been *fxd*, and admired her trim, unused vulva that always kept her sort of a puppy, and inhaled her furry, spongy tartar smell. I rubbed her tummy until she relaxed and went limp and trusting the way she used to, with me, her little almond-shaped eyes closing in warm, sleepy peace, and I knew she loved me again and she knew how much I loved her. She let her head drop back, and the soft, clumped curls along her throat weren't any problem at all, because I'd been very, very careful to sharpen the blade.

I'd bought a new ball to put in with her, but afterward I realized the rubber wouldn't burn, it would just melt to a smoky, periwinkle-blue lump in the fireplace. And the aroma of her was so good, like rich, roasting, crackling kernels of popcorn. So I just buried the ball in the backyard. Sometimes now I awake alone in the middle of the night, thinking I hear its *thump-roll*, or feel her shove it under my thigh: *You want to play with my ball? Here, look, here's a ball! You want to play? Please, please! Please, please, love me love me love me.* Sometimes I hear her nail-scrambles on the floor.

I just wish I'd tasted her before she burned all away. I'm sure she would have tasted so sweet. Like apricots.

BAKERY GIRL

There are two kinds of women here: the old ones, wrinkled and chipper, with hairpinned buns or permed wisps, knobbed knuckles and grandmother names like Ruby, Esther, or Bess, who work the morning shifts and slice and bag marbled ryes with the efficiency of nuns. And then there are the girls, in their mid- to late teens, who come in after school, if they go to school, to relieve the old ones. The girls work till closing at 9 PM, and all day Saturdays and Sundays. The smell of their fruity lip gloss and gum competes with the cherry-topped cheesecakes and yeast, and they cinch their bib aprons tight around their waists, tug them low over their tank tops, lean far over the counters toward the rare male customer. The old ones have been working here fifteen, twenty, thirty years and greet regulars by name, know their preferences in rugelach; the girls are just passing through, they tell themselves, just picking up the minimum-wage pay-check on their way to something better, something else.

The new girl is watching the other girls. She is the young-est one here. Her mother, purchasing Sunday morning bagels (two raisin, two egg), had offered her up to the boss, a fifty-something aging rocker called Elliott, son of the shop's origi-nal owner, an octogenarian for whom the bakery was named. Elliott appraised the girl, took in the pearly-pink nail polish, the good posture, the evidence of pricey orthodontia in the awkward smile. It wasn't quite legal to hire her. But he likes the younger girls, they work hard. And the customers would like this one, too, her baby fat and still-clear skin. The older girls, well, they start to look a little tough after a few years. The divorced mother liked the idea of her daughter working in a bakery, a Jewish bak-ery at that, such a wholesome, homey place, the greeting whiff of sugar and butter and dough. And she'd know where her daughter would be on weekends and in the afternoons, while she was at work herself, brokering foreclosed condos.

And all the sweet things you can eat, Elliott had told the girl, grinning, and she'd smiled back.

There are also two kinds of men here besides Elliott. The Latino guys who load dough into kneading machines and bake sheet after sheet of cakes, and the descendants of the original owner, a flock of male cousins in their late teens and early twen-ties who carry trays of cookies and loaves back and forth. They all look like younger variations of Elliott. All of them are musicians. During their breaks they sit on the hoods of their cars in the parking lot and play air guitar. The hottest of them, an older girl advises the new girl on her first day, is Jamie, Elliott's son. He actually plays in a band. His girlfriend's pregnant, but everyone thinks he shouldn't marry her and get tied down just now. None of the girls like the girlfriend. She's a bitch, they chime in, overhearing. Jamie's really hot. Check out his car. A repo'd Hummer he got from a police auction, he jazzed up the rims, put this velvet all inside, painted it black. Maybe she can come with them to see him play sometime. We'll sneak you into the club.

The new girl nods, happy. These girls are much cooler than her friends at school. She's never had access to girls like this, worldly and mature. She is just barely filling out her A cups, so she tries to keep her shoulders back, her chest muscles outthrust. She has had nine periods in her life. It still thrills her, the surprise warm curl of blood pushing through to her underpants, the buying of junior tampons, the womanly tug of a cramp. When she masturbates, reading at night from her mother's nightstand books, there's more wet and a sharper smell now, her insides get to a harder clutch and peak. And now she has her first job. All the sweet things she can eat. Friends who go to clubs. Girls who know about sneaking you in, who use gloss, not balm, who laugh like women. Things will start to happen now. She's not quite fourteen.

HERE, LITTLE ONE, Kate says to her, handing over a brown paper bag. Could you slice this for me? Kate is the oldest of the young girls, twenty-one, with black liner shaped like fish around her eyes and a cracked front tooth. Elliott has assigned Kate to train her and has been keeping an eye on them. *Watch and learn,* he'd told her. Kate calls her Little One, compliments her handling of napoleons and squeezes her arm warmly and often in praise. Kate is one of the nice ones.

Sure, she says, agreeable. She is still learning the machines, how to slice breads and seal up cakes in pink cardboard and string. She likes the job, most of it, likes being helpful to customers while Elliott nods in approval. She likes the coating of sugar on everything, the sweetness whenever she licks her lips, the stickiness of fruit fillings clotting her hair and the smears of buttercream she finds dried on her face and arms. She keeps her hair in two braids, seals the ends with twist-ties they use to bag challahs; when she gets home at night from the bus stop, smelling of onion and fudge, she unripples her hair and appraises herself in the mirror, deciding her fatigue and sweat and hurting feet and, yes, is that a pimple, her first?, are signs of maturity, of growth.

She reaches into the paper bag, feels an odd thing, pulls out, what? A rubbery, peach-colored club, double-knobbed at one end. It feels tacky, smells chemical, like petroleum. It is sinister, somehow. She is humiliated by the thing, fat in her hand, but isn't sure why, doesn't know why she feels a twisty flush between her legs. She smiles uncertainly and hears the other counter girls crack up.

She's never seen one before! Kate announces.

A little big for her, don't you think? Maria says, to more laughter.

Another thing she has learned: not to trust these laughing girls. During her fifteen-minute break on her second day, Denise had asked if she wanted to see her modeling shots, then shown photos of herself splayed naked in a garage on top of a stack of tires, her mouth gaped wide and her fingers pulling her vagina open and raw, and everyone had laughed at her startled face. Shelley had asked if she had any blow and snickered when she'd stammered an offer to ask around for some at school. Nicole wanted to know how many guys she'd fucked, or had she still only done oral? Monique offered to fill her in on all the cousins and back-room guys, then described each of them by the size, shape, and smell of their cocks, that word, said over and over, hurting her ears. Debbie advised her to start early on anal, your hole can take it easier when you're young. They bring the reek of cigarettes and beer back into the bakery after their parking lot breaks, despite Elliott's rules. They tell bumper sticker jokes: *Bakery Girls Knead It. Bakery Girls Cream Their Pans.* She has wanted to cry several times, has comforted herself with mouthfuls of the broken Danish and cookies the girls stuff as they please, with big bites of marzipan to get the ache out of her throat, with sucking stray buttercream frosting from her fingers when no one is looking.

And now she holds the dirty rubber thing in her hand, ashamed of feeling ashamed. She somehow knows what the thing is but can't quite form the word in her head. She suddenly hates her two baby braids. They are all laughing, and she wishes she could scratch at all of them.

Leave her alone, come on. A guy comes out from the back with a tray of prune homentashen, and all the girls suddenly grin, stand up straighter, or strike an exaggerated slouch. This must be Jamie, she thinks. He has shaggy blond hair, dark blue eyes that are kind, teeth that look brushed. He smiles at her, and she thinks of her father, how he used to take her for Sunday breakfasts at IHOP, just the two of them, before he left, and let her drown pancakes in chocolate sauce and whipped cream.

Fuck you, Jamie, I'm supposed to train her, Kate says.

Yeah, I know how *you* want to train her, Kate, says Tim.

Yeah and how *you* want to watch, Kate says. Catcalls all around. Kate grabs the dildo back, pokes it toward Tim, who slaps it away.

Jamie leans close to her as he slides the homentashen into the display case. They're assholes, he whispers. Don't let them get to you, right?

No, she says, uh uh.

Good girl.

He winks at her as he heads in back, his empty tray gleaming like a shield against his chest.

I LIKE YOUR car. She has been practicing these words in her head for weeks, waiting for the perfect moment when the others aren't around, when Elliott isn't eyeing her, when his girlfriend, Fran, isn't nearby whining about what time he's going to get off work, her hand protectively held over her still-flat stomach. His schedule is a mystery, so she lip-glosses now before every shift. She lingers to admire the car on her way in to work, on her way home, whenever it's there and the cousins aren't around to hoot at her, always hoping he might suddenly exit the bakery, see her, offer to take her for a ride. It gleams like the shiny black part of a black-and-white cookie. He hasn't spoken to her again, just smiled in a friendly way with those pretty bright teeth, those starry eyes, and once he tugged on her braid—just one now, down her back, more grownup—when he passed.

And she has him now, by the bread bins, he is all hers, his smile and his tray of loaves hefted high.

Yeah, thanks, he says. It's okay. I can haul my speakers and shit, you know?

Maybe, she says, maybe I could come hear you play sometime. Everyone, everyone says you're really good.

Oh yeah? he says, pleased. Sure. Sometime. Not on a school night, though. He winks at her again. Through his T-shirt sleeve she can see the hair under his arm, dark blond curls, as he swivels to go.

Fuck school, she says, surprising herself.

Yeah? he says. He stops, lowers his tray. I thought you were, like, a bookworm.

No way, she says. School sucks. She leans casually against the slicing machine, tries to slouch. I can't wait until I'm out of there, you know?

Oh yeah? he says. He taps his tray, grins at her.

So yeah, like, anytime. I mean I could do anything, anytime. She's pleased to hear herself say all of this, doesn't know where these words have come from. I mean like now, she continues, I'm on my dinner break. She unties her apron strings, pulls it over her head, hangs it on the rack. She straightens up, glad she wore a thin T-shirt, one that clearly reveals the seams of her bra. I'd love to see your car.

Okay, he says, nodding. Sure. C'mon. He heads in back, and she follows. Her heart is happy. She will sit next to him in his velvet and black car and he'll tell her about his music and how Fran is such a bitch and all his secret things, they'll go have a cheeseburger somewhere and talk more, they'll come back to finish their shifts and then later he'll play guitar for her, drive her home even, no more taking the bus. She feels Elliott's eyes on her as she follows toward the back exit. But Jamie stops at the chiller, unlatches its heavy door, and disappears inside without looking back. She is unsure for a moment what to do, nervously picks at a kaiser roll on a tray until she sees Elliott return to squirting out a pink basketweave design on a baby-themed cake.

She enters the chiller, startled as always by the slap of syrupy cold. Jamie is standing just inside; he holds out his hand and she gives him hers, still sticky from the strawberry tart she ate earlier. His hand is warm. She hopes she smells like strawberries. He tugs her past a tall rack of wedding tiers awaiting their roses, toward the far corner, behind stacked tubs of hydrogenated oil, and turns her to face him. Kiss me, please, she wants to say, but tells herself to just wait, that's what he's brought her in here for, isn't it, to kiss her first? She licks her lips. He unbuckles his belt, unbuttons his jeans with one hand and places the other one on her shoulder. He wants her to kneel, she realizes, so she does, her jeans too tight around her belly, her knees, she feels her house key dig into the tendon of her crotch. Too many cookies, she thinks, I'm getting so fat. She's suddenly worried he'll touch her, hug her, he'll hate my body, he'll think I'm ugly, too big, too small, too flat. She closes her eyes and turns her face up, waiting for the kiss, his mouth, his tongue in her mouth, that's what she wants, his clean toothpaste tongue and his detergent sugar smell.

She feels a bump at her lips and she opens her eyes. Rubber, that's all it is, peachy and soft, but no, it's real, a real kind of flesh she's never seen, and she swallows. She tries to think of the right word for this, there's only *penis* in her head, the only word she can say inside, but *penis* isn't right, it's like Biology or Health, the kids at school, they'd say *dick*, but that's a stupid schoolyard word, there's *member* from her mother's books, she had to read those paragraphs a few times before she realized what a *member* was, not *dildo*, either, and this one's real, warm, there's a pulse, and hair, and an oniony human mustard smell. There's just the other word, a word she can't even shape in her head, let alone her mouth, she can't get her mouth around that, no, not this wordless hot soft hard thing, but she opens wide for the thing she can't say, feels him enter her dry mouth, pressing her dry tongue, it grazes her teeth and she instinctively opens more, feels him fill her then bump at the back of her throat, and she somehow gasps and swallows again, with him all in there, full and hard, her throat opens and closes around him, and he says *Yeah*. He slides out, then, *Lick it*, he says, and she's empty and sad but does, lapping at him and around and around with her tongue, then he pushes back in full, slides out, slides in, It's his *cock*, she thinks, *yes*, and the wet of her mouth makes the cock slide good, easy and slick in and out, glosses her widened lips, makes a slopping sound, makes her wet and loose all through, she feels the pounding not in her filled mouth but between her legs, that's what's empty, throbbing inside and damp and swelling up hard. She wraps her arms around his hips, lets him push in deeper, go faster, makes herself wider-open for him, for his cock his cock his cock and oh, he's mine, he's all mine and I'm all his, his, his.

Good girl, he says, his hands closing soft around her head, pushing her toward him with his slide, slide in, slide out, gently, he is so sweet, she feels him slide all out and suddenly be gone from her and it aches. But he raises her up and back and now she is seated on big sacks of meal. His hands are tugging on her T-shirt, twisting it up, she feels him dig inside her bra, her little-girl baby bra, she is so embarrassed, stiffens her spine, thrusts herself outward into his hands, they're gripping her breasts, squeezing the flesh hard, *Bakery Girls Knead It*, yes, yes, her bra up around her throat as he grips her nipples, they're raisin hard and chilled, he rubs at her, and she lifts her face up to him for his mouth. He pulls her back toward him, puts his cock, his cock, shiny slick from her mouth, tucks it between her breasts, pointing up at her, pushes her breasts closed around it, They're too small, I know, she thinks, despairs, wants to apologize. But *Sweet*, he says, makes a sandwich of her with him the meat in the middle and her the tender soft rolls, he starts shoving, rubbing himself hard up, up, up, gripping himself tight with her breasts and she wants his hands other places, wants them squeezing the crotch of her jeans, wants them unbuttoning her and reaching down and in to touch her skin, her baby belly, her hot wet hair, wants his fingers spreading her open and raw, going inside her, groping there the way she does it to herself, rubbing the tiny hard spot then sliding fingers inside then doing both at once, rubbing, sliding, all the wet coming like a swell and burst of steam. Another hard shove rub and he clenches tight inside himself, clenches her hard, and she feels his gasp, the hot ribbons of him on her throat, her neck, her chin, she opens her mouth and swallows swallows and licks at it, gulps it down, gulping, hungry, it's all hers, and then she's suddenly released. She steadies herself against the meal sack. She wipes at her face, wipes her hand on the burlap. She hears a buckle. She feels a tug on her braid.

Your break's almost over, babe, he says. You go out first.

She leaves the chiller, and the hot blast of the baking room turns all the wet and damp to stale sweat. She doesn't want to go out front, not yet. She leaves through the back exit, into the parking lot, and there are no cousins or girls around. The bus stop is across the street; she can feel her house key in her jeans pocket. She feels a buttercream smear start to crust on her cheek. She can feel getting on the bus and going home by herself, letting herself into the empty house and taking a hot shower and going to bed, curling up in her ballet-pink sheets, although it's only seven-thirty, too early for bedtime. A shaft of sunset hits Jamie's car, turning the shiny black a sudden hot white, and she floats her hand along the brilliant passenger door. Her reflection is a blur of a girl. She takes the key from her pocket and heads back inside to the bakery, running the key hard along the edge of the car as she goes.

WIG

The long black hairs on the white tile look like a child's wild scribbles, each strand a separate graphite scrawl. I think that I should sweep them up. Save them for something. Didn't women used to do that, save their hair combings? To make padded wiglets of their own hair, robust false curls? In high school we'd used those long black strands of her hair for dental floss after lunch. It was that strong. That healthy, that thick. She always had the prettier hair. A thick, glossy black, while I had to blow-dry and torture and gel for an angelic or Botticelli effect. I would've killed for her hair. I sat behind her in Algebra and made long, tiny braids of it, like those bracelets of black elephant hair, like shiny jute. At the beach she'd coat her dark hair and skin with sunscreen, her melanin-rich, impervious skin, while pale blonde me slicked on the baby oil to get a glow going, heedless of burn or the later shredding I'd do. We took tennis lessons together, and I was the better player—I had to win no matter what, heaving, jolting off oily sweat with each lunge—but she enjoyed it more, was beautiful with it, queenlier, fat black ponytail swinging, moving serene as Greek or Egyptian royalty in the sun.

It should have been me.

"You don't have to do all that," I hear her call after the toilet's second flush.

I should get her a glass of juice, maybe crackers, sometimes that helps. I'm desperate to do something for her.

"Shut up, please," I yell back.

"I don't want you doing all that."

"Remember my sixteenth birthday?" I yell. Me falling down in the cantina bathroom, her shoving fingers down my throat so I could vomit up the cheap, fruity tequila, her lifting my limp bangs from the bowl, her giving me cupped palmfuls of water, her wiping flecks from my mouth. I owe her. I rinse the basin again, wipe it with a fistful of tissue.

"Hey, it's what friends are for," she calls. Weak.

"Exactly. I just wish your aim were better."

I hear her try to laugh, and I marvel, again, at how she's bearing this. But the energy's got to give out soon.

The air in here is still rank, despite my double flushing and basin rinsing and healthy blast of pine. Despite the bathroom's cheery mess of little boys' bath toys, the husband's rosy *I love you* card masking-taped to the medicine cabinet. I examine my own healthy, guilty glow in the mirror. Twenty years' exposure, and my price is just a minor epidermal leatheriness. My own hair is still a natural blonde, even at thirty-six. Just helped out a little. A few chemicals, and voilà, I'm still blonde as sixteen.

I evaluate my eyebrows; the one very dark brown hair beneath the right brow arch, the one that always grows in fast, is poking its way back. Her wild eyebrows will probably start slipping away now, too, bristly hair by hair by hair. I find tweezers in the cabinet, pluck, and toss my tiny whisker in the sodden-tissue trash. I get down on my knees and pick up her thick, long black hairs, hair by hair by hair, and bury them deep in the sodden-tissue trash so she doesn't have to see. She shouldn't have to face that, yet.

I look at my own fair face one last time in the mirror, next to the *I love you*. It really should have been me.

WE GO SHOPPING for a wig. It's time, she'd said. I don't like scarves, I'm tired of scarves. They're too resigned. Come help me buy a wig.

I'm a little surprised by this; a wig seems, well, dishonest, and she's the most honest, artless person I know. No makeup or plucking. Those heavy black eyebrows, too thick and undefined. Not a woman to wax or bleach or shave anything, to moisturize or scent. Her husband impressed me on this. I'd watch him run an affectionate hand across her hirsute shin, playfully tweak her armpit's floss, lovingly tease her for the faint mustache dusk on her upper lip. She wound up winning a prince of a guy, sensitive, devoted, stroking, the kind who sticks it out. Maybe it's ironic, now that she's getting barer every day, the follicles giving up. Now that she's getting fairer, wispier, her skin going bruisable and fine. Soon she'll need to pencil in some brows if she wants them at all, but I imagine she won't even bother. I would've expected those straightforward scarves from her, maybe some baseball caps, honest and resigned. But she wants a wig, and of course I want her to have whatever she wants, whatever makes her feel better, and I want to be with her through all of it, it's what friends do, so we wait for a day her energy's up, and her husband is crazy busy at work and her boys are at school, and we go.

But we can't find the right one. We go from shop to shop to shop, from Hollywood to Pico Robertson to Encino, smiling at balding old ladies and transgendering people and other translucent-looking women in scarves. She's flagging but determined, and we learn a great deal about wigs. She immediately rejects synthetic hair for its artifice—I say nothing to what seems like a mild hypocrisy—and for its lesser durability, although an impassioned, eager-to-instruct Salesguy in an upscale West Hollywood boutique assures us a good-quality synthetic can last two years with the right care. This moot, insensitive question of *durability* hangs in the air a moment, and I say nothing to that, either, but agree she should go for human. We learn there are four basic kinds of human hair—Chinese, Indian, Indonesian, and Caucasian—and we learn that Indian and Chinese hair, because of its strong nature and thick diameter, is able to undergo harsh chemical processes to make it smooth, shiny, and tangle-free *Processed Hair*, but that the most glorious hair, the only kind, really, we should be looking at is *Virgin European*. We learn that wig companies send employees out to remote villages or mon-asteries or convents in Russia and Italy to contract for hair; the hair-growing people must agree to always keep their hair pro-tected and safe from pollution and sun damage, to never blow-dry or style. The wig people then return years later to harvest the crop with razors or close cutting at the scalp. This all makes me slightly queasy—it sounds too much like people stripped naked and yielding, handing something precious over to someone else with questionable or inhumane intent.

She finally finds one she likes, a bright auburn, Pre-Raphaelite mass, kidney-length and decadent, with a hand-tied, monofilament top. I'm stunned by her choice. She takes off her scarf to try it on, and the exposure of the holdout black hairs on her tender white scalp makes me look away in pain. The Salesguy is talking passionately about ear tabs and cap size and maybe the need, soon, for special Comfy Grips to hold the wig in place against a smooth dome of bare skin, You know some guys, he tells her, when it's time for a piece, they actually have snaps surgically implanted in their scalps to hold it in place, can you imagine? and I finally look. She's smiling, but I don't think it suits her at all, it's too outrageous and it doesn't work with her olive-going-yellow skin. But she's excited by it, turning to see all angles of her head, flipping the tendriled ends behind her, and there's no point in being honest at a time like this—let a little denial grow, I think. The bravery'll have to crack, at some point. I tell her she looks beautiful. Go ahead, I say, you look like a Russian empress, a queen, and, when the Salesguy nods agreeably at that and she hesitates, looking all at once timid and drained, I say,

"Do it. Be unabashed, be bold."

She smiles at that, then:

"I'm worried. . . . " she says.

"Don't be," the Salesguy says. "With that face, that bone structure, you can pull anything off."

"What are you worried about?" I ask quietly, and the Salesguy, sensing a new level of intimacy, squeezes my arm, nods, and discreetly moves away.

"You want some Compazine?" I offer.

"No, I'm okay, thanks."

"So, what?"

"It's been awhile," she begins.

"Since?"

"You know. Since." She pulls panels of long red hair down in front to cover her breasts, Godiva-like. I've noticed her breasts have been going limp. Everything about her is losing tone.

"*Since*," she repeats.

"Oh." I look away to examine a bottle of wig shampoo. "Maybe that's just normal slackening off," I suggest. "Two kids, married eight years. It's nothing, it's totally normal."

"I'm not talking slackening. I'm talking a real while. Like being cut off."

"Maybe he's worried about hurting you," I suggest.

"Maybe."

"Maybe he feels guilty," I say.

"Guilty for what?"

"Oh, I don't know." I don't know what to say. "For not being able to fix things."

"Maybe."

"Maybe he's got stuff going on, too," I say. "He's going through this, too. He needs taking care of, too."

"You're right. You know, why don't you come over some night? We can just hang out, watch a movie or something. The three of us, like we used to. Before all this shit."

"Sure."

"And he's been working such crazy hours. I'm almost feeling like he doesn't want to be around me. Maybe he's grossed out."

"You're being ridiculous. He adores you."

She tugs the wig further back on her forehead. "Does this look natural? Or just whory? Tell me the truth."

"He loves you, you know. He couldn't care less."

"But do you think he'll like this? Come on."

"It's great. He'll love it. He loves everything about you."

She nudges me her thanks, gets out her wallet, and I applaud her. She's paying and I'm smiling, stroking her new marrow-colored curls, but all I can picture is some peasant or nun shorn of her hair, her naked baby-bird head bent low over bills for oil or coal, counting the coins for a new church bell, a new milk cow, medicines for the orphans, loaves of black bread, all so my friend can entice her husband, cling to illusion, grip at fading hope.

But then I listen carefully to the Salesguy's complicated instructions about styling and cleaning and care, because I know that, although her husband is such a prince of a guy, this exhaustive task of tending will probably fall to me. It's what friends are for.

DO IT, BE *unabashed, be bold.*

I don't remember which of us said that first. We all used to say it to each other, back when they were dating and they'd include me, we'd hang out and get a Meat Lovers' pizza, rent a movie plus two sequels at a time, get stoned and drunk on scratch margaritas and tell ourselves we hadn't yet outgrown a single impetuous thing. Then after, when they got married and they'd include me, we'd hang out and get a cheeseless veggie pizza, watch movies, get selectively stoned or drunk, then soon-later-after, when they had kids, the first boy and then rapidly the second one, and they'd include me, and we'd put the kids to bed and hang out, eat the kids' leftover canned ravioli off their plates, watch TV but not get stoned or drunk anymore, because the kids might need something and we all needed to keep it real.

Then the weekend, a year or so ago, before *all this shit,* when she and her kids went off and away to her mom's for the weekend and one of us called the other one, I don't remember which, it would've been so normal either way, *Let's hang out, get a pizza, watch a movie.* I probably was the one to call, actually. I was being a good friend, I was worried he'd be lonely all alone. And the getting stoned on a forgotten, leftover ziplock bag in the freezer and drunk on vodka and kiddie apple juice just seemed to follow, seemed natural, too, although it had been a long while. And then cracking up, being too silly, the playful shove-touching we always did and then not so playful, and then groping and stroking as it all of a sudden went rash, and then just doing it, being unabashed, being bold. Waking up the next morning, in her sheets, one of her long, healthy thick black hairs stuck to my right breast, like a reminder to floss. *Let's forget this ever happened, It doesn't mean anything, Doesn't count, Yes, I love her, I love her, too*, batting clichés back and forth to each other and spraying the fetid air with pine. *We can't ever tell her, Not ever, Yes, I love her, I love her, too,* and both of us feeling so, so sick with it.

I'll never tell her. She shouldn't have to face that now. She deserves it all to be as pretty and clean and normal as we can make it.

A WHILE LATER, she changes her mind. It's trying too hard, she says, it gets in my way, falls into food, the toilet, the boys keep tugging at it. She's back in a scarf, she's shrugging, resigned. The wild red wig is carefully rewrapped and back in a box; she's donating it to a special group that gets wigs for poor women and kids.

"It just wasn't me," she says. "It just didn't work."

"I thought you looked beautiful," I tell her.

She bites her lip, looks out the car window.

"He didn't like it?"

She shrugs.

Maybe he's not the problem, maybe it's you, maybe you're the one who can't handle losing your looks, not him. I think this, but I don't say it, I loathe myself for the mere thought.

"So, right, we'll keep looking," I say. "It's a quest. We'll find the perfect wig."

I picture some twelve-year-old girl with leukemia wearing the donated wig. Some little girl who'll never get married or have kids, never get laid or kissed, who'll probably be buried in that mass of whory *Virgin European* hair.

"I appreciate your doing all this with me," she says, quiet.

"My God," I say. "How many places did I drag you to find that horrible pink dress?" Twelve stores. I was desperate to find the perfect dress for our senior prom, consistently unhappy with the look of my pasty arms, my negligible breasts, my pastel hair, my washed-out skin tone. She drove us around from place to place in her mother's gassy Toyota, the patience of a saint, encouraging me, all the while looking perfect in the first thrift shop dress she'd found, darkly glamorous next to her perfect boyfriend of the moment, me going with his irrelevant best buddy, by default, actually, she'd arranged it so we could all be together. We took a group photo, camera snapping at the exact second I looked at her burgundy satin and thought, *That would have worked on me, better on me, she should have offered to swap.*

In a Miracle Mile shop that markets to Orthodox Jews she finds a simple, chin-length brunette bob, sleek on her, actually, more sophisticated than her own old ponytail and bangs, and I'm shocked at the price—it's a chunk of money I'd expect her to put in her boys' college fund, not blow on vanity, on a lie of hair. But she raises her thin, sketched-on eyebrows at it, too, shakes her head.

"Such a pretty girl," the Saleswoman says. "*Shana punim.* What a shame."

"Will you just go on?" I tell her. "Write the check—you deserve it."

She glances nervously at the Saleswoman.

"Oh, well, you have insurance?" the Saleswoman asks. "You can get a prosthesis prescription, you know."

"Too late for that," my friend says. "I already blew it."

"Well, it's a lot, I know," the Saleswoman says. "But it's like buying a car. You can buy a Chevy, or you can buy a Cadillac. It makes all the difference."

My friend just gives her a wan, brief nod.

"Okay. That's fine, I'm going to let you two talk about it. Such a face . . . such a face deserves the best. Tell you what, dear, I'll take off twenty percent if you want it, make it a sale price, all right? You let me know." The Saleswoman veers off toward a young, bewigged housewife in a turtleneck and lisle stockings, carrying a bakery box.

"You look very elegant," I tell her. "Sleek."

I can see the pulse in the sad, stark vein on her temple.

"Listen, why don't you let me chip in?" I say.

"Oh, please. No. Thank you."

I can see the tremble to her sallow chin. "Are you tired?" I ask. "How about something to eat? Should we get you a snack?"

"I'm not hungry."

"You want some juice?"

"Stop babying me," she snaps.

"I'm sorry," I say, taken aback. "I'm trying to help."

"No, I'm . . . " She takes my hand; hers is looking like an old lady's, waxy and clawlike. I wonder if she's toxic, if the chemicals can seep out of her pores to poison all the innocent people around her.

"I'm not used to the role reversal, you know?" she says.

"It's okay."

"Thank you for being so patient with me."

I take my hand away to fuss with a wigstand. It's a wire armature of an empty and featureless human head, like the model for a cyborg.

"I'll just get this one," she says, tired. "It's fine. It's nothing. Really, it's fine."

"Good," I tell her. "You're a Cadillac, you know," and she smiles.

YOU'RE SEEING SOMEONE, *aren't you?* she'd said to me those months ago. *You have that glow.*

Not really.

Come on, tell me the truth. My life is so boring.

So I made up a story, because she knew me too well, could probably smell it on me, a story to throw her off, *Yeah, some new guy, but we're keeping it just casual, nothing serious, nothing worth talking about. Don't you think I'd tell you if it were anything real?* I pointed out.

Damn, she said. *I'm dying at least for something sordid.*

It doesn't even rise to the level of sordid, I told her. *Sorry. It's nothing. It doesn't even count.*

So, yes, it went on a while, a little thing that took surprising root. Shaving my legs and puffing my hair up wild every day and keeping a fresh sweep of makeup on, trying to get to and stay ready and perfect, in case he called to say he'd found us some time. He found it now and then, and I got good at patient. *Just until it's out of our systems*, we assured each other, *It'll die a natural death and everything will go back to normal.* And *We'll never tell, it isn't even anything to tell. We'll spare her.* Until the mole took us all aback. Until that once-teasing wink of a birthmark on her brown thigh abruptly went lethal and foul. *We need to stop, now, We need to think of her, now, yes. Be there for her. Let her have both of us, all of us.* Both of us avoiding each other, now, we can't even bear to be in the same room with each other, it's too intense. Only happy smiles now, for her, and being the prince of a husband and the beloved best friend in the world we're supposed to be, being there and keeping it all caring and real, for her.

WIG #3 IS a Farrah-esque blonde romp.

"Does this look like I *know* it's retro?" she asks me. "Or like I don't get the joke?"

She strikes a Farrah pose, head tilted back, a manic, toothy grin. We're back on Hollywood Boulevard, in a place where all the wig styles call movie stars to mind. There's also the "Halloween Line": witches, vampires, Elvira, Rainbow Clown. Can I have you today? she'd asked on the phone. Can we have a quest day? Let's go out in search of. Be silly. Play. She's between courses and has had a renewed burst of energy, a manic, zenith buzz. There's a glow from her skin, and I wonder if she's radioactive.

"I wonder if it comes with the red bathing suit," I say. "And the nipples."

"Those, I really do need. Mine have snuck back inside somewhere. Like turtles."

"What kind of nun did *this* come from?" I ask the Salesperson.

"Now, that one's a human-synthetic blend," he tells us. "Good value for the price. Look at the rich tonal dimensions of color-play. You only get that with natural." He fluffs the wig's feathered waves.

"So . . . it's a *natural* synthetic blonde?" I ask, and she laughs.

"No, you never get those highlights with synthetic. It's the human hairs that do it. Of course, they've been chemically processed to get that color."

"Chemically processed," she repeats. "Boy oh boy, can I relate."

"But this hair is still cuticle hair. Still high-quality. Now, a blend like this should last you two or three years if you're lucky."

"Listen," she says, "*I'm* not going to last two or three years," and we both laugh. Her days are numbered and look at her, laughing. I'm edgy with the counting down. I'm too aware of waiting for the egg timer to ding, for it all to be over and done with.

"Right. Excuse me." The Salesperson leaves to help a dowager-humped woman with wisps, waving at him from across the store.

"What was wrong with the kosher one?" I ask.

"I don't know. It was too plain. Too serious."

"Too severe?"

"Yeah. I want to play a little. That one didn't make me feel . . . fetching."

"You think he'll find this one fetching?"

"I don't know. He's always liked blondes."

I put down a blond Afro wig to look at her. "He's told you that?"

"A million times."

"That isn't very nice, to tell you."

She shrugs. "Doesn't bother me. It's honest. One of his best qualities. Honesty."

"Really?"

"Sure. Don't you think so?"

"I think you can be an honest person without being honest about every single thing that comes up. Little things that don't do anything but hurt someone."

"But that isn't hurtful." She shrugs again. "Just honest."

"Sometimes being a little dishonest is the kind thing to do."

"But I think that's what's held everything together for us. Especially through this shit. Knowing everything. Knowing everything's been said. Shared. I think it'll make it easier for me. And for him."

"I suppose. So, well, okay, he likes blondes, huh? I didn't know that."

"Always. Always had a thing for blondes."

"Yeah, well. You won."

"Won?"

"He chose you, I mean."

"Right. He chose me. But he didn't choose all of this." She gazes in the mirror, shakes her head so Farrah's blonde swirls go mad as foam, then settle. "Eighty-seven days and counting," she tells me.

"Are you kidding?" I say. "Is that all? It's been longer than that for me."

"What about that guy from a few months ago?"

"Yeah, exactly, *months* ago. We broke it off. I mentioned that."

"Oh, honey. I'm sorry." She looks upset. "You seemed hopeful about him."

"No, I didn't. It wasn't anything. It was complicated."

"Well, maybe down the road, you guys. Maybe it was just the timing, then—"

"It didn't count. I told you that."

"I'm sorry." The look of compassion on her face is a look I've seen before. It's the look when I'd score the point, I'd win, and she'd be the one to kindly, misplacedly ask if I was okay, how was my ankle doing, the blister on my thumb, did I need some water, did I want to take a break?

"Let's just forget it," I say.

"I guess I've been pretty self-absorbed, huh?"

"That's okay. If I had any stuff worth telling you about, I'd just tell you. Your stuff is more important."

"Yeah. My eighty-seven days. And I've been feeling good. The last week or so. I've been doing so well. Don't I look good?"

"You look great. You look beautiful." It's a lie, she doesn't, but I say it to make her feel good. "All your color's back. It's like you're all back."

"Let's go get pedicures. Eat cheesecake. Play tennis. Let's find a river to skinny-dip in."

How sad, I think, that this is the extent of her imagination. That she can't see she's on her last gasp. It *is* her last gasp, after all, I remind myself. It's just a matter of time now, after all. I unclench my fists. I tell myself to get back to patience. To pity.

"Whatever you want," I say. "But you need to make a decision first."

She glances around the store. "Maybe the Veronica Lake. Or the Marilyn."

"The Shirley Temple? The Dolly Parton?"

She looks at me, smiles, looks away. "I've always wanted

blonde hair, you know," she says. "I guess I've always had a thing for blondes, too."

That fat black ponytail, swinging.

"All right, fine, just come out and ask him why. Ask him why you guys aren't doing it anymore," I say. "Make him tell you."

"Maybe."

"If honesty is so great. Go on. Ask him to tell you the truth. See what he says."

"Yeah. . . . Okay, here's honest." She faces me. "I'm going to be honest with you."

"Oh, please don't." I laugh a little.

"Really. I want to know everything between us has been said."

"Are you sure?"

"I've always envied you."

"Why?"

"I've always hated you, just a little. For your hair." She flips a lock of the Farrah at me. "Really. The attention you always got."

"That was you. You always got the attention."

"The blondes-have-more-fun thing. The fairy-princess thing. Guys and blondes."

"You're deluded. You're the one guys have always gone for."

"I mean it. Envy. Hate. Because of your hair. Ridiculous, but there, true."

"Well, I don't know what to tell you. Maybe yours will grow

back in blonde," I suggest. "It does that sometimes, right? Grow back in completely different?"

She just shakes her head, gives me a knowing look.

"Yeah, well . . . mine's chemically processed now, too," I remind her. "Mine's all a lie. You'll have to find something else to hate me for."

IT'S A SHOCK to see her back. Or, almost back. The long, straight black hair, the bangs. No ponytail, though, because time's up, the nadir is here to stay, she's mostly back in bed and reclined now and it would make the back of her head hurt. She found it online, she tells me, the perfect reincarnation. It was easy to order, she knows all about *Virgin European* and cuticle shaft by now, knows her cap size and her need for Comfy Grips. She shows me every tiny detail, the hand-knotted wefts and the latex scalp textured like actual skin. I expect to see a dandruff flake, a blocked pore, but no, it's perfect. And she was lucky, it was the last one the company had in stock and they sent it express.

"What do you think?" she asks, proud, hopeful.

I get a whiff of her, a fake sweetness on top of the other smells. She's wearing perfume, as if that will help. "I suppose I'm a little hurt," I say. "That you went ahead without me. I thought we were a team."

"Oh, honey," she says. "I couldn't ask you to keep questing with me. You've done way too much. You've been so patient, so amazing."

"Well, it looks great. You look exactly like your old self," I tell her. "You look like you're sixteen." She's pleased, in a weak but self-satisfied way, and I remember the day in Algebra, we had a midterm but the night before we'd stayed out late, some retro film festival midnight show, and she'd made up some story for our aging, stubby teacher. I remember his rapt, understanding face, his devoted gaze as she told him whatever lie she'd told, tossing me into it, too, winning him over, me standing behind her and her thick black curtain of hair. She won us both an extension, bought us both more time. She was always able to get whatever she wanted, and I'd get the surplus by default. Just by hanging around her. Just by waiting things out.

"So, I've been wanting to ask you something," she says.

"Sure."

"It might sound weird."

"Go on. Ask me anything."

"What do you hate me for?"

"What?" I say, startled. "I don't hate you for anything."

"I told you. I got it out of my system. So come on, I need to know. If you hate me for anything. If there's anything you've never told me."

"There's nothing."

"There must be something. Twenty years? Be honest."

"Okay," I say. "I hate you for all of this shit."

She smiles. "That's too easy. We all hate me for that."

Just then her husband comes in, bearing a tray of yogurt and sliced fruit, a glass of juice. A tight bud of a rose in a tiny crystal vase. He is hesitant, I can see him ostensibly focus on not spilling anything.

"Sweetheart, can you eat a little?"

"Sure, I'm hungry." She nods in my direction. "Hey, she says I look like I did when we were sixteen."

He smiles at her, but not at me. "I bet that's true," he says to her.

"It is. It's the truth," I tell him. "I'll show you a picture sometime." I fluff my hand through the top of my hair, where it feels flat.

"Oh, I believe you." He carefully rests the tray of food on the bed next to her, fussing so that he doesn't have to meet my eyes. I understand he needs to be careful, but I still think about some way to get him to look at me, face me. I just have to wait, the moment'll come. He's being cautious, but he won't be able to help himself. It's been so long. We've been so patient. So good. But there's a sudden loud blast of cartoon music from the other room, and little-boy voices getting combative.

"Hey, you guys," he yells, "keep it down."

"No, let them," she says. "Just let them."

"You should take a nap soon."

"I will, later." She spoons yogurt into her mouth. "We're talking about stuff."

"I'll clean up before I leave," I tell him.

"No, that's okay, thanks, I'll get it," he tells my general direction over his shoulder. "And you need some rest," he says to her. He leans over, brushes the fake bangs back, kisses her on the forehead just below the start of fake scalp. Right in front of me. As if I'm not even there. He isn't avoiding me, I realize. I'm just not quite anything. I don't quite count.

"Yeah, I'm taking off soon," I say to his retreating back. "Don't worry."

"Here." She offers me a spoonful of yogurt with a wavering hand. "I really can't eat this. He's trying so hard, I don't want him to know."

I take the spoon, hesitant to put my mouth where hers has been. "What is this, vanilla?" I say. "Ugh. Just eat what you can, I'll flush the rest."

"He's a prince," she says. "He really is."

"Yes," I say.

"So we made love last night," she tells me.

"Oh?" I say.

"I thought at first it was just guilt, or pity, you know?"

"Yeah, maybe."

"But I really think it just hit him that there needed to be a last time. Where you *know* it's the last time. So you'll always have that."

"You think that was the last time?"

"Yeah." She takes a bite of a slice of nectarine; her fingers are shaky and she puts the rest down. "It wasn't good the way it used to be good," she says. "I mean, it used to be *great*, you know?"

"Yes," I say. "I've heard."

"But it was good for all the other reasons it stays good. I mean, it was awkward and uncomfortable, you know, it's been a long time, but then it had all the things you always hope will be there between you. Like it's just the two of you in this moment, this space, but in a way that will last. Something you'll always have. I hope *he'll* always have. I hope he'll remember that part of it forever and forget everything else. I think he's hoping for that, too. I think that's why he did it." She laughs, sheepish. "Or maybe it was just a pity fuck."

"Yeah, maybe," I say. I don't know how he could stand the smell of her, the chemical sweet trying so hard to cover up the waste and rot.

"Or maybe it was just the wig." She strokes her beautiful long black hair. "You think?" she asks.

I see his mouth still pressed to her waxy, wasted face. I try for patience, for pity. For sparing her.

Do it, I think. It's what she wants. What she deserves.

"You really want me to be honest?" I say. "Really honest?"

"Yeah, of course. Thank you. What?"

I have her full attention.

"We slept together. A couple of times."

She looks at me, her face blank.

"Months ago. Before all this."

There's a raw twist and crumple to her features, and I feel a joyful rush, a jolt, the lunge for the ball you just know you're going to smash back hard and win the game with, the thing that'll let you win the prize, be victorious and serene.

"You were off at your mom's with the boys, and he thought we'd just watch a movie, get pizza. Like the three of us used to do."

"I know," she says.

"except you weren't there, you were gone—"

"I know, stop,"

"and he invited me over, and—"

"I *know*," she repeats. "Just *stop* it. Stop."

I stop.

"I don't want details," she says. "That's between the two of you."

"What are you talking about?"

"He told me."

"He told you."

"Last night." There's the crumple of her again, beneath the glossy bangs, then she takes a breath and her face settles back to smooth. "I knew something's been wrong. I knew there was something. What you said before, about him going through stuff, too, remember? So I told him whatever it was, he better be looking at the clock, you know?"

"And he told you."

"It wasn't easy. It wasn't pretty. *I* wasn't pretty. Believe me, you would *not* have wanted to be here for what was going on last night."

"No."

"But finally, finally, I was all right. It was horrible, but afterward, it was all right. It was good. The two of us. I think it's even why it was good." She actually laughs. "Well, that and the wig."

"What about me?"

"Oh, honey." She takes my hand. "I was hoping you'd say something. That you'd be honest with me. I'm glad you told me. I've always been able to trust you that way, how you don't leave things unsaid. That's what I need now. You get to this place where, if it isn't real, forget it." Her face is fully content and peaceful now. Her face is a plastic, placid mask. "And hey," she says. "Don't think this is weird, but I even had the thought that maybe you two would get together. Afterward."

"What?" I say. "Excuse me?"

"I know, weird, fucked up. But in a way, it makes sense."

"Are you kidding me?"

"He'll need taking care of. And the boys. And it would be all right with me. If that happened. Because it doesn't change anything. I want you to know that."

Like some queen granting favors, tossing coins to her servant girl, bread to the peasants, giving her lesser jewels away to charity.

I see his sensitive, devoted hand ceaselessly on her leached-out skin, her toneless body.

Caressing her glorious, extravagant, interminable hair. Stroking her, undyingly.

It really should have been me.

" . . . yeah, maybe this really did the trick," I hear her say.

There's a chuckle. She's fussing with her wig, she's been talking this whole time.

"All the others were a lie. Trying to be someone else. This is really what I wanted."

"This one is perfect," I tell her. "It's you. The perfect you."

"I want to be wearing it, you know. In the box. Promise me?"

"I promise you."

"And you have to check my eyebrows are all right."

"I promise. The eyebrows, and I'll be sure you have it on."

She examines a lock. "I got yogurt in it. I want it to be all pretty and clean. You'll make sure, okay? Even when it gets crazy?"

"Give it to me now. I'll wash it now. We have that special shampoo." The clock is ticking, I think.

"You don't mind?"

"Please," I say. "It's what friends are for."

"Would you close the door? The boys . . . " She fusses with

her Comfy Grips and gently slips the wig off with practiced care. "Going out in style," she says.

She hands it over to me, carefully, and I picture the remote, yielding nuns surrendering their precious and painstaking sacrifice. She's all stripped down to scalp and skull now, illusionless, fetal and wizened. She's no empress, no Cadillac, no queen, just a drained sack of festering skin and I'm the only one able to see it, spot the patches of sweat on the burgundy satin dress, really know the ugly, bald truth about her. She's hideous, but everyone else will eternally see only the beautiful fake. I imagine her lying serene in her casket, flushed clean and perfectly groomed, an abiding Nefertiti or Cleopatra.

"Be careful," she says.

Do it, be unabashed, be bold.

"I promise," I repeat.

I take the wig into the bathroom with me, close the door. I run the water in the sink. I open the medicine cabinet, still and forever announcing *I love you*, find the tweezers. I close the toilet lid and sit, cross one leg over the other, take her hair in my hand, her perfect and healthy and human black hair and I begin to tweeze. I pluck each thick, glossy fake strand out by its fake root and let them drift hair by hair by hair down to the cold white tile floor.

THE KNITTING STORY

She knits as a clumsy, pudge-fingered child, because her mother loves to tell her the once-upon-a-time story of knitting socks for her college boyfriend, painstaking argyle-diamond wool socks for the princely young man who carelessly thrust his foot through the sock toe after all that labor the mother did to show and prove her love, because that was how. She knits because her mother is at a luncheon or antiques show or mahjongg and Can't the child occupy and entertain herself, and so after school the child trudges to the craft shop and spends her allowance coins on a *Let's Get Knitting!* booklet, and fuzzy pink yarn like a long bubble gum worm, and a pair of pointy twig-thick needles she is a little frightened of, because if you walk around with them and trip you could poke out an eye, and on the floor of her canopy-bed bedroom she teaches herself how to *cast on*, how to loop little nooses of yarn through other loops, scoop the alive loop through and let the old loop fall away and die, loop loop loop, your rows like little crooked corn fields growing, and then you *cast off* and are done and look what you have made and can do, ta-da!

She knits gifts for her mother—a potholder, a hot pad, a long tubular scarf, everything a wormy fuzz pink—because that is how, and her mother exclaims with joy at their sweet misshapenness and spills bloody meat juice on the hot pad and scorches the potholder and cannot wear the scarf because of its so beautiful but impractical color but is so very proud and What else can the child make, What else can she do?

She knits because she grows absorbed by the taming of chaotic string into structure, the geometry of a messy line turned to a tidy grid, and her fingers slim to deft and she buys slenderer needles and more elegant yarn and her after-schools and weekends are now so very busy herself, in her room with all those squares. Square, square, square, a big gifty pile of them, this is what she can make and do.

She knits because it is precious of her, because grown-ups find this little knitting girl adorable.

She knits because her best friend in high school has prettier ringlet hair and wears girlier, more impractical shoes, and so she teaches her best friend how to cast on and loop loop and cast off, and they both make the now-perfect potholders, the precise hot pads, the scarves that lie flat, and then the best friend goes away to an expensive college in an icy state and returns at her first Christmas holiday with magical sweaters, glorious garments with plackets and cables and set-in-sleeves and stitches like vines and popcorns and the holey appearance of lace that everyone goes *ooh* and *aah* for, and the best friend explains it is not enough to just *Let's Get Knitting!*, the same childish stitches over and over again for row after row gets you nothing but a pile of meaningless squares that no one wants or loves, you must follow a pattern in order to create an actual *ooh* and *aah* thing, and she is angry and ashamed the prettier, better-shoed, and effortless-at-everything best friend had understood this and she had not.

She knits to perform the trickery with cable needles and yarn overs and ribbing and moss stitch and basket weave. She knits to tame sloppy loose skeins into tidy submissive balls in her hands, at her feet. She knits to exhibit mastery. She knits in public, at coffeehouses and airports and parties, her crafty hands blurred with speed, and people look in approving wonder at her industriousness, her occupying and entertaining herself, her un-idle hands, no lazy devil's handmaiden, she.

She knits because she can rip out what is imperfect and do *frogging*, the unraveling of the completed or semi-completed thing to an again loose scribble, because you *rip it rip it rip it* out, like the *ribbiting* frog, who is only an ugly sticky frog and not the perfect prince and then you can start all over.

She knits because her kneaded dough will not rise into a proper loaf.

She knits because it frightens her to read.

She knits because she doesn't understand calculus.

She knits for the first grown-up man she falls in love with, a damaged man whose flattering cruelty sends her to study a library of patterns, swatch multiple yarns, debate even in her sleep the best fiber content and thickness, because the right sweater will heal him, the correct cotton merino or cotton cashmere or cashmere merino blend will basket-weave and moss-stitch and cable this man to her, the ribbing will cleave him unto her and keep her at his side, because look at this, her handmade healing labor of love, so she obsesses over this yarn's slight scratch and will it irritate him or keep him sensitized to her, or that yarn's lack of elasticity and will it make of her precious gift a saggy and shapeless thing? She knits because his flattering cruel attentions are trickling hourglass sand, his growing coolness stiffens her fingers, and so she knits faster and even faster like the princess in the fairy story who races to knit sweaters out of stinging nettles for her twelve beloved brothers turned into swans from a witch's curse and thus turn them back again before they are stuck that unmanly swan way forever, knitting with bleeding fingers to save them into complete-again princes by this show of her love. She knits feverishly, her fingertips pricked into splits, but the sand-gritty time's-up man carelessly thrusts her away before she can finish the last magic stitch, like the fairy-tale princess ran out of time and had one sweater with only one sleeve for the swan brother who would now be stuck with one wing instead of an arm forever, and she is consumed with guilt and fury at her failure to craft the perfect healing thing in time, and so she frogs the finished sweater, erasingly, wishing a witch's curse on him, an eternal hair shirt of stinging nettles, a next-in-line indifferent and cruel woman who will brutally cripple and leave him an open, forever-after wound.

She knits wedding-present blankets for fiancé'd friends, the Victoriana-flowered or fisherman-Aran afghans to adorn the feet of marital beds or drape across the Mission sofas in the den or warm their couples' embrace. She knits to soak the DNA from her sweaty fingers into their lives, as they TV cuddle or fuck or share nighttime tales of their tedious stitched-up lives.

She knits because she doesn't like the smell of children.

She knits because she is afraid of her career.

She knits because she is not allergic to cats.

She knits for another man, who is gentle and loving and neither frog nor prince, and she grows impatient knitting for the pattern of his gentle lovingness, she knows nothing she knits will shape him well or into the right thing, so she stealthily unravels her work by night like Penelope's secret unweaving to forestall the choice of a suitor, but by day she keeps on knitting for the gentle loving man, because that is what you do, that is how. She knits like the spider at the center of the web disdains the ensnared fly even as it feeds, she knits in her mind while the gentle loving man makes love to her and she comes only when she imagines herself stabbing her shiny needles into his soft flesh, into the wet, submissive ball of his heart, and so she hurries to cast him off and away before she destroys him with her hateful, unmagical knitting for real.

She knits for pregnant friends' future joys, knits whimsical pea pod snugglies and pumpkin hats and the treacle-pink or frozen-waste blue or gender-neutral blankies to be soon covered in apple juice vomit and leaked urine. She knits for the *ooh* and *aah* baby shower moment of applause, and then it is time for the next, less-wondrous gift to be opened, and she knits to pity them all.

She knits while watching a television program about people who choose to be cast away on a desert island and contest with each other in mock tribes to remain there, cast away and useful to their tribe in some mysterious strategy for survival, and she knows she would knit hammocks from palm frond strings so everyone might sleep hammock'd up and away from the sand fleas and snakes and rats, she would knit to keep everyone else clothed, she would knit nets to catch fish, and then when all her tribal friends were well slept and fed and clothed and warm, they would cast her away, cast her off, throw her in a volcano and be rid of her forever.

She knits vests for the shivering, soapy penguins newly cleansed of oil spill oil, because she is nurturing.

She knits sweaters for the naked baby pandas in a Chinese zoo nursery because she is internationally engaged.

She knits a cardigan for her elderly father, who is already shrinking and shivering inside his closet of clothes meant for a full- and warm-muscled man, but she knits slowly, for she knows once the sweater is finished he will be, too, so she knits stitch by stitch as if patiently teaching a clumsy, pudge-fingered child she doesn't have, until there are no more stitches to stitch and she wraps her father's loose bones in the sweater and buries him in it, because that is how.

She knits security blankets of bargain-bin yarn for home-less abandoned infants, because she is maternal.

She knits chemo caps soft as kitten bellies for brave, hair-shedding friends with translucent skin, because she is support-ive and merciful.

She knits because studies show knitting reduces the risk of dementia, and she will not become a fogged, unraveling person who must rely on mocking, merciless tribal friends for survival.

She knits until her hands are swollen and carpal tunneled into witchy old-lady knuckle knobs, into burning nerves. She knits into numbness, into scrim.

She knits and knits like Madame Defarge in her chair, con-tent in the breeze of the guillotine blade, knits until she feels the blood has risen warm to her ankles and it is suddenly, surprisingly, her turn now, sees she has blindly knitted herself into the wooly smothering thing that will bag her own cold, twiggy bones, and that is all she has ever made, or done.

STAPLES

My boyfriend's other girlfriend is at his home in his bed right now, with staples in her scalp. This time was a brow lift. The doctor slit her scalp from ear to ear at the hairline, hitched up an inch or so of face and forehead, and stapled the skin seam shut. My boyfriend demonstrated this to me in the Japanese restaurant, sliding his hands across my own scalp, under my hair to the roots, my ears mashed flat against his palms. He made *kachunk* noises as he pantomimed the stapling. Then he blew a strand of my hair from the manila folder next to his plate of sashimi. He'd called that afternoon to tell me to meet him, that he could get out for a few evening hours, that I should wear a shortish skirt, and that I should download the treatment for his new screenplay he'd attach in an e-mail, take it to the copy place, and bring him ten copies of it at dinner. The manila folder holds the original. He gives the copies to friends, for feedback. Right now, his girlfriend thinks he's copying. She's lying in his bed, swollen, bruised, in pain, icepacks chilling the tiny stainless-steel clips, thinking he's off at the copy place to make ten copies of his treatment, but instead he's eating pricey sashimi with me, stretching the smooth skin of my face up by my ears and hair to illustrate her, and making loud *kachunk* noises as he knuckles a stapled line across my scalp.

On the floor next to me is the stack of treatments. Also, a plastic grocery bag. He'd called me back to tell me to pick up a few things. After the copy place, he'd told her, he would stop at the market. I was to pick up milk, bread, orange juice, broccoli, cooked chicken breasts from the deli counter. Everything organic. Toilet paper. Whole-grain bread.

Oh, and fruit, he'd called back a third time to whisper. She wants some fruit. Don't worry, I'll pay you back.

That's okay, I whispered back, I have to go to the store anyway.

I didn't want my dad to overhear I was doing this, buying groceries for my boyfriend. He's never liked my boyfriends, but I know it's just paternal gut reaction, all the worry. It isn't that he doesn't trust me—I've had his Visa card since I was fifteen, he trusts me to be smart and use it wisely for whatever I need, that I won't abuse the privilege.

I shift away and twirl a finger at the waitress, indicating

I'd like more sake. My boyfriend is twenty-six but always gets carded. I never do, for some reason, although I'm only almost twenty-one.

I wonder if the girlfriend will like the organic Fuji apples I selected, the juice with calcium and D and extra pulp. The expensive, brand-name juice I always buy for her. My boyfriend never keeps these kinds of things in the house on his own, for himself or me, only for her, for when she comes to town to get work done, and then to him, to heal. She lives near San Jose with an eight-year-old daughter she'd had on the teetering edge of being too old, and after acting failed, whom she refuses to raise amid the glitz and decay of Los Angeles. The daughter, my boyfriend has told me, goes to stay with her father when the mother is here, the ex-husband. The mother has been here a total of twenty-three weeks in the past two years, I calculate, the same two years I've been with my boyfriend, to undergo then recuperate from the work on fatty eye deposits, liposuction on tummy and hips, collagen injections, breast augmentation, facial chemical peel, and the current brow lift, which means the little girl has spent those same twenty-three weeks with her father, the ex-husband. I feel sorry for the little girl, her mother leaving so much. But it's probably a special treat to spend that time with her father. I imagine he takes her on Ferris wheels at carnivals, clumsily braids her hair and ties bows, makes sure she washes her neck, holds her hand when they cross the street or go for strolls to get ice cream, tells her how wonderful and pretty and smart she is. The special kind of father stuff.

Meanwhile, my boyfriend icepacks his girlfriend's body, changes gluey dressings, washes her rank hair in a basin, and gently feeds her the bread, orange juice, and fruit I buy. He watches over her full time, devoted, and slips out to spend little gaps with me. When she's healed enough to go back to San Jose, her daughter, and her current business venture, the last of the fruit will rot and the bread will grow mold and the juice will ferment to foam, and my boyfriend will return to me and his screenplays and his staples of beer and salsa and fried pork rinds for protein. He will spend a portion of the money she leaves him to stock up on margarita mixes, frozen pizzas, and canned cream soups and bank the rest. He keeps blue icepacks stuffed in with the frozen burritos and quiches and taquitos. It's the kind of food we eat when I go over to his place, and I often wonder when that diet is going to kill him. But when she's in town, and giving him extra money, he spends much of it taking me out to pricey dinners.

A couple of years ago she bought a pair of thigh-high leather boots, a boned spandex bustier, and a studded crop and placed an ad in the local paper. Silicon Valley guys called, lined up, became regulars, and she rose a tax bracket. But she got tired and worried about keeping it all up. She started getting work done, the minor nips and tucks, the same kind of work she'd eschewed when it might have helped an acting career in L.A. but now, well, her options were narrowing and she needed to make the most of what she had.

I don't judge her, I had said to my boyfriend when he told me about her. She has a daughter to take care of. Food, clothing, rent. Life's expensive. You do what you have to.

Exactly, he'd said. I keep telling you that.

The waitress brings another warm white bottle, and I pour.

So, she's taken it online, he tells me tonight. Given she wasn't actually fucking anyone anyway, you know? Customers e-mail requests, she links up maybe a dozen or so who want the same thing, just acts it out live online. She doesn't even have to see these guys. She's making a shitload of money. For just mind-fucking. Boilerplate B and D. The Come-to-Mommy crowd. No real fluids, no real skin.

So, why is she still getting all this work done? I ask.

He shrugs. Hey, even online she needs to look good. Who wants to get tied up and spanked by some old pig?

He tells me her website address, in case I want to "check out the competition."

Yeah, right, I say. Gross.

He laughs. You have nothing to fear, he says. Hey, did you get a receipt?

He's caressing the manila folder, and I realize he means for the copies, not the groceries. He can write off copies.

That's okay, I tell him. My contribution to the arts.

God, you look pretty tonight, he tells me. He tugs my face over to him by my bangs and one ear lobe, gives me a kiss. I love you, he says, but it's the tugging that hits home.

He asks for the check he's going to pay with her cash, although I've been thinking I'd like to order more, and at the same time asks the waitress to give his ticket to the valet. He likes the car out front when we leave, waiting for us, when his girlfriend is in town. This gives us more time to park someplace— I can't exactly invite him back to my house. I'm still hungry, the sashimi didn't fill, but I don't want to be selfish about his time and I can't stay out too late either, or I'll just get hell. I gather my jacket, my purse, my copy of his treatment, and watch him count out twenties like playing cards.

Don't you . . . feel sort of funny? I ask, because I've always wanted to ask and right now I finally can't bear not to, I feel too humiliated for him, sleeping with this woman old enough to be his mother, this woman who's just using him.

About what?

Letting her support you.

You're one to talk, he jeers. Still living at home.

Wait, I'm still going to school, I point out.

Yeah, and I'm still working on my script.

It's completely different.

I know. Sweet deal you've got.

He thinks I'm spoiled, but I think it's perfectly normal for people to live at home until they finish college.

It's not that great, I tell him. Believe me, the second I graduate, I'm out of there.

Right. He looks at his watch. You're probably at the library right now, huh? He winks at me, leaves with the groceries and stack of treatments, knowing I'll follow. Knowing I'll hurry.

We park on a side street and make love with the steering wheel jammed against my back. I look down to see where we're joined, but the pleats of my skirt have fanned out over us. It's my old plaid skirt from private school, my little-girl skirt, the shortest one I have. I move it aside to see, and my boyfriend palms then grips the insides of my thighs, digging in with his thumbs where it's soft. He's pushing hard, everywhere, and I start to come, and I think about the girlfriend's little daughter. I hope she got a good dinner, too. I hope her father took her to a real restaurant, not fast food. Or that he made her something nutritious, balanced, all the basic food groups represented. The milk, the whole grains, a protein, a fruit. Organic.

I wonder if my boyfriend's girlfriend ever questions how he spends her money, or what he does when she's not in town. I'm coming and feeling bad for her, lying there tonight in all that pain and waiting for him to finish at the copy place. I wonder if tonight she'll question why he smells of fish.

WHEN I GET home, I hurry straight to my room, wary and quiet and carrying my shoes. I'd told my father I'd be studying for midterms at the library, I'd be home late. The first few years after my mother left, I was eight or nine, and we were left alone together, he was always so nervous, so worried. He wanted to do everything right, be the perfect parent. Make a good home for me, make sure all my needs were met, give me lots of quality time. He was always careful I was eating right and getting my vitamin C, *No candy before dinner, baby, here's an orange,* and *Finish your milk, okay?,* that he'd covered me tenderly and well in high-SPF sunscreen, that I had a full bath every night, *Did you do your homework, don't lie to me, now,* that I brushed my teeth before bed. I was the first of my friends to get her bedroom all redone the way she wanted, to get her ears pierced, to get her own computer. He bought me a car when I was sixteen and gave me a credit card for gas. But he was so strict, suffocating, had all those rules, *As long as you're living in my house . . . , I'm the parent, you're the child . . .* or he'd get angry, grill me about where I'd be and with whom, *Boys only want one thing . . . ,* and always wait up for me, *I want you home by eleven from now on, I want you to always tell me if anyone ever pressures you to do anything you don't want. . . .* But I realized it was just because he cared so much. He wanted to keep us close, connected. And I proved myself so trustworthy over the years, got such good grades, was such a good girl, did everything I was supposed to, that he finally relaxed and eased off. He pretty much lets me come and go as I please now, thank God, hardly ever questions me anymore.

Like tonight. His bedroom door is closed, the light is off, but I tiptoe anyway, tiptoe past in a nervous rush.

I promised my boyfriend I'd read his treatment when I got home, but I decide to read it tomorrow, when I'm clearheaded. Instead, I go online and bring up the girlfriend's site.

I'm on vacation, my babies! it announces. *But here are some favorites to keep you happy until I return!*

Just for logging on as a *Visiting Guest*, I can see a gallery of still photos (*Freebies!*) and a five-second loop of flicking tongue, leather-strapped breasts, an open-thighed flash of groomed red pubic hair, vivid, moist-looking skinfolds. I look for staple scars or needle marks or lingering bruises from previous work. I think last time was the breast job. Not to make them larger, he'd told me; to make up for the breastfeeding, pick them up a little. She'd had her nipples regrafted and reangled higher. I look for tiny Frankensteinish stitches around the areola. I peer and try to zoom in on the stills, but I can't get close enough. The upturned breasts look beautiful. She looks beautiful. It all must have hurt, but there's no pain on her face. She looks much younger than how old I suspect she really is. I can't imagine how the current brow lift can make her any better. I didn't know she was a redhead. I wonder if the daughter has red hair like her mother, too young for armpit or pubic fuzz, sure, but sweet, long little-girl red hair, strawberry or ginger, always smelling of sunshine and sunscreen and soap.

It's $21.95 a month to become a member, an *Elite Guest*, which allows me access to community chats and restricted live videos. An *Exclusive Guest* ($49.95 a month) gets personal, virtual shows and *Very Personal, Very SPECIAL Hands-On QUALITY TIME!* with her. I use my father's Visa and sign up with what I think are masculine-sounding initials.

Thanks, honey! comes up onscreen. *When I'm Back In Town, You And I Will Spend Some Very, Very SPECIAL Hands-On QUALITY TIME Together! Meanwhile, You Be A Good Boy!*

If my father notices the monthly charge on his Visa, I'll tell him it's an educational thing. An online listserve for research, or maybe a special kind of virtual tutoring. He'll be happy I'm doing that, he'll be very proud. I graduate next year, I'll have to figure out what kind of lies to tell him then. I'll need good lies, so he doesn't worry, so he doesn't get all upset.

THE TREATMENT FOR my boyfriend's new script has story problems, all his friends except me seem to agree. Some holes, some loose ends, the inciting incident needs punching up, the second act drags. I thought it was wonderful, perfect, I told him I loved it just as it was. I always think his stories are amazing, but he never believes me, or he's never satisfied. He went back to do more work on it for weeks and weeks, consumed and not seeing me, and finally finished what he now calls a ready-to-go-to-script treatment. Attached it to me in an e-mail: *Can you read this asap, I need your feedback!? And take it to the copy place, make ten copies, please, please?? And come over to my place tonight, you pick up dinner, I'll do hors d'oeuvres, I love you, yeah?*

So? he asks. I've brought chili cheeseburgers from Tommy's, his favorite; we're eating them sitting on the carpeted floor of his studio apartment in the Hollywood Hills. It's a converted garage, really; the actual house belongs to a ninety-six-year-old former bit player, who still lipsticks her mouth to look bee stung and uses his rent to buy food. There are green-furred oranges on the kitchenette counter and a white-furred heel of whole grain bread. We have old *Varietys* across our laps, under our burgers and microwaved mini-chimichangas and dim sum laid out on the abandoned screen door he uses as a coffee table. The only other place to sit is the double futon, but it's lumpy, unmade, and unlaundered, and we'll wind up there anyway.

So? So?

So, it just gets better and better, I tell him. The story is wonderful. It feels so real. You're absolutely ready to go to script.

I should just throw it away and start all over, he says.

He looks morose, opens another beer. After getting the copies and the cheeseburgers, I'd stopped to pick up the imported kind of beer he likes, a brand from some former Soviet country.

I should just burn it, he says. Put it through a fucking shredder. He kicks at the stack of copies I've brought. I hate that fucking story, he says.

No, you don't, I tell him. If you didn't still care about it, you wouldn't be so upset.

I reach over to pat him, soothe him, but he jerks away.

You don't know what you're talking about, he says.

I know that you're talented and you're creative and you're disciplined, I say. I wish you believed me. I wish you believed in yourself more.

Jesus, he says. Well, hey, thanks for reading it, anyway. Thanks for taking the precious time away from your precious fucking schoolwork.

I've been available, I point out. You're the one who's been preoccupied.

He eats the last dim sum, scrapes up chili with a finger.

I made an apple tart for dessert, I tell him. Will you eat some? Or we can split an orange?

He doesn't answer; I get up and find most of a gallon of chunky skim milk in the mini-fridge. I'd like to throw it away, scrub dried spills from the sink. I'd like to clean his toilet, vacuum the gritty blue shag carpet, but don't want to make him mad.

You don't eat enough fruit, I say.

Fuck off, Mother, he says. He eats the last mini-chimichanga, rubs his hand on his shirt.

You need the vitamins.

Unbelievable.

I just worry about you, that's all. I care. I love you.

And that's what you think love feels like? he says. But he's smiling, and I know he actually thinks I'm wonderful, that he needs me for this, he just doesn't know how to say it, how to express it.

So, are you at the library right now? He reaches over to slide his dirty fingers through my hair.

No, I'm studying at my friend Stacy's.

Do you have a friend Stacy?

No.

Wow.

He moves aside the used, chili-stained *Variety*s and pushes me flat on the floor. I've been wanting and waiting for this for weeks, it feels like it's been a long, long time. I flatten out for him, spread all open, and he starts making love to me, but it's so gently I can barely feel him there. I try to get into a tighter angle, so there's some torsion, some clash, but he adjusts with me and it's all too smooth and loose. He strokes my face, he's being so sweet, and I'll never come this way. I need the edge first, the clench of muscle, before I can go slack. Maybe he's worried the floor is too hard, maybe he's worried about hurting me by accident. I nod my head at the bed, and he slips out to let me go first. We lock in again and keep going. Now he's stroking my hair, so I cross my wrists overhead and nudge them under his other hand, hoping he'll grip them hard, give them a twist. I push my head up under his stroking hand, hoping he'll grasp and tug my hair, make me strain. But he seems to want us even, balanced, and I just give up. I let him gently lunge and stroke away, and watch the square of paneled ceiling, the rustle of the jumbled sheets. There's a stain on the pillowcase next to my head, the kind of leak a thin brownish fluid might make. I wish I could get up and wash all the linens. But not to wash away any trace of her. Just because I don't like the thought of him sleeping in soiled sheets.

BY NOW SHE'S soaped herself up and given me, or the masculine-initialed me, a virtual bubble bath; squatted over the camera and peed to virtually spatter me; squirted lube on her fingernail-filed hand and pantomimed a good reaming; had me tie myself up at ankles and wrists (hard to do); assigned me a variety of punishments involving food or lack of, or sustaining physical positions; told me to lick her boots; acted out giving me an enema; pretended to apply alligator clamps to my nipples; cracked a leather riding crop at what's supposed to be my ass, my scrotum, the tender soles of my feet; mashed her breasts into the camera and told me to suck; told me to call her Mommy; told me I'm a bad, dirty little boy. She's played with herself and taunted me with shiny fingers, told me I'm not allowed to touch, mustn't touch Mommy, bad dirty little boys aren't allowed to touch. She's a good actress, but I find it all very unengaging, and I'm bewildered there are guys willing to pay for such things. I'm bewildered there are guys who are turned on by this. I've logged on once or twice a week, very late at night when I'm sure my father is asleep, for my *Very SPECIAL, Hands-On QUALITY TIME*, and I keep looking for more of her, trying to get her closer. At first I thought I saw swelling from the brow lift, maybe the barest puncture marks from the staples along her hairline, but she's been wearing bangs and I can't see much. Otherwise, she looks exactly the same as she always has. I'm at a loss for what else to request, how to keep it going. The degradations, the hurts, the playacting—it's all getting so lackluster, so old.

Hi, honey, she says to me. She's sitting spread-legged on a chair, her red hair tugged into a bun, a gladiator-sized leather belt across her waist. Long black gloves.

Hi, Mommy, I type back. I type with one hand, I'm eating an orange with the other.

Have you been a good little boy? Beneath the bangs, she raises her eyebrows at the camera, and I wonder how she can still do that after the brow lift.

Yes, Mommy, I type.

Oh, you have? And what have you been up to? she asks.

I can't think of any scenarios. It's very late, and I'm tired. I spit a seed out of my mouth onto a paper towel. Too tart, the acid first, then some sweet.

Are you sure you've been a good boy? Or are you lying to me? she prompts.

No, Mommy. I wouldn't lie to you.

Well, I think you are lying. And I don't like it when you lie to me, you know that, don't you? It hurts when you lie to me. She looks severe and yet, I realize, caring. Incredibly sincere. She cares a great deal whether I've been good or bad. And when I'm bad, it causes her pain.

Yes, I'm sorry. I'm lying, I've been bad.

Well, you know what that means, don't you? She frowns, and I'm in thrall to her again, at what she must go through. *You'll have to know how much it hurts. You'll have to be punished. But because I love you so much, I'm going to let you choose.* She rises from the chair, opens a small cabinet that holds a variety of props. She removes a round blade of wood, like a pizza slide, like a large Ping-Pong paddle. *How about this?*

Spank me, Mommy. Of course, I think, we haven't done that. So obvious. Why haven't I just asked for that before?

Ah, she says. She puts the paddle back. *That's Mommy's favorite, too.*

She comes closer to the camera, slowly removing the gloves. She sits so that she's only visible from the waist up, murmuring to me to drop my trousers, drop my underwear, lie down across her lap, *That's a good boy, no, a little higher, Mommy wants this bad little boy's sweet behind a little higher*, and I split open another orange. I hear a slapping sound, she must be whacking an open palm against her own thigh, just out of view. I spit out another seed—the problem with oranges, you have to fuss with seeds, with drip, so sticky, my father would always make me wash my hands afterward. The girlfriend keeps slapping away, *This is good*, and I wonder, for the first time, where the daughter is while her mother does all these shows. The late-at-night shows, she's probably sleeping, sure, but what about during the day, when she gets home from school? And how does her mother explain all the equipment, the cabinet with the paddles and crops and enema bag? Has the little girl ever stumbled into this stuff, this special room, by accident? *Here, let me stop, rub you a little, good.* And did that make her mother angry, that her daughter maybe broke a rule, did something she wasn't supposed to? I wonder if the mother disciplines her daughter, not like she disciplines her clients, of course, but she probably spanks her now and then. That's part of being a parent. Part of being the child. Maybe the little girl's father, the ex-husband, is in charge of discipline. My father was, even before my mother left, he was usually the one to handle spanking. *Now that doesn't hurt too much, honey, does it? Maybe I should do it harder, then, like this?* I imagine the little girl's father stroking her hair, kissing her, telling her he has to do this, punish her, she's been bad, telling her to pull up her skirt, pull down her panties, lie across his lap, just like my father. *Like this, this?* I've finished the orange but my hand is so sticky, I have to lick each finger one by one. Bent over his lap in a tense hunch, crying, at first, everything clenched, panties around my ankles like soft rope, the jolting slaps like awful gripping sunburn, like growing blaze, *Believe me, sweetheart, this hurts me more than it hurts you,* me crying and pleading, my body giving up into a drape, but he'd finally stop, when I was finally beyond hurt and fully loose.

That's good, that's my baby, yeah, she says.

My hand sticky and acid-wet, rubbing with her, rubbing faster, my eyes on the ceiling, hearing her slaps, she's breathing hard and I'm breathing hard and then *Now, yes, yes.* I look at her then and see the sheen on her upper lip, her perfect, chemical-burned upper lip, they were right, it does hurt them more than it hurts me. Then candy, then ice cream.

Thank you, Mommy, I type.

My pleasure, baby, she says, sunny.

Then the screen goes blank and a message comes up: *I'm Going On Vacation, Honey! When I'm Back In Town, You And I Will Spend Some Very, Very SPECIAL Hands-on QUALITY TIME Together! Meanwhile, You Be A Good Boy!*

ISN'T SHE FINISHED yet? I ask. I move aside the plastic grocery bag of skinless chicken breasts, broccolini, whole-grain pitas, fruit, and skim milk and sit closer to him in the booth.

She's a work-in-progress, he tells me. He leans past me to riffle in the bag. Oh, shit. I forgot to tell you. No more dairy. She's switching to soy.

I'm sorry.

That's okay. I can stop on my way home, I guess.

We don't speak for a moment, just eat our pasta primaveras without garlic, our salads with fennel and grape tomatoes. I'd ordered a forty-dollar bottle of Pinot Grigio, and we drink it.

So, I say, what's she doing this time?

Tummy tuck. The liposuction made her pretty saggy. Although she says it was even like that before, from having a kid. He glances under the table, at the seat to the other side of me. Hey, didn't you get my e-mail?

He has abandoned his old treatment, started all over again, same story but a completely different take. I'm realizing, I think, that this is what he always does. I wonder if he'll ever be ready to go to script.

Yeah, I got it. I printed it out for myself, but I had finals today, I couldn't get to the copy place. I'm sorry.

Shit. I'm supposed to be copying right now.

I'll go tomorrow. Maybe I can drop the copies off at your place?

Excuse me?

Oh, yeah. Well, maybe you can get away and meet me tomorrow afternoon? Or tomorrow night?

Maybe. It depends. I'll just do it myself. He nudges me with his elbow. How'd your finals go?

Okay. They're over. Just one semester left.

Yeah, congratulations. Then it's welcome to the real fucking world, kiddo.

I know.

Wait'll you have to pay bills. Wait'll you have to find a decent place to live.

Fine by me. I can't wait to get out of there. I'm so fucking sick of being treated like a kid.

He shrugs. You just don't appreciate what you've got.

So, what did they do to her? I ask.

It's like this . . . he leans over and reaches under my shirt, trying to pull up a handful of belly flesh. It's like they squeeze as much of her stomach skin as they can get. . . .

He pulls, and there isn't much to grab, so it hurts. But I like the hold he has on me.

. . . and they staple it like this—he makes those *kachunk* noises—she's got these dozens of staples all across her gut. He finishes *kachunk*ing across my torso. And they cut off all the extra.

Won't that leave a scar?

She says she can wear a belt over it or something. And you can rub vitamin E over the scar so it won't be so bad.

You didn't ask me to get any vitamin E.

You do that later, after they take the staples out. Right now her stomach's all puffed up, like she's pregnant. She looks like shit. And it hurts, she can barely move.

Right now I'm out celebrating finals being over with my friend Stacy, I tell him.

Yeah?

I can stay out pretty late.

Yeah, listen . . . I actually better get going soon. No dessert, even.

What do you mean?

I'm sorry. But now that I have to stop at the store and everything . . . and she's in bad shape this time, I probably need to get back. . . .

Oh.

He lets go of his grip on my stomach to scoop up the last of his pasta.

Come on, no big deal. You look like you're going to cry. I need to take care of her, all right? Don't be so fucking selfish. She's really hurting. You want to be a big girl about this, or what?

I DECIDE I might as well stop at the copy place tonight, maybe he'll be able to slip out for breakfast tomorrow and wouldn't it be a good idea if I had copies ready for him then. The treatment for his new script is twelve pages long, and the original has been cut up into pieces and scotch-taped and paperclipped back together—I don't want to trust the counter guys to do it right, so I grab a key for the self-service machines and stand in line with my manila folder. Although it's almost midnight, there's a long wait. The whole mall is busy. It looks like half of Los Angeles is out strolling in couples or having coffee at the coffee place, ice cream at the ice cream place, or in here copying their screenplays and treatments. I glance at the pages of his treatment as the copied pages collate, wondering how he's changed his story, but I'm thinking about the girlfriend, how she keeps coming back and back and back for more work. How much more of herself she can replace, shore up, wire together? I marvel at what she's putting herself through, how she can keep standing all the pain, how worth it it all must be.

I finish at the copy machine and go to the central table for stapling. I staple and staple, still thinking about the girlfriend at his home in his bed right now, with all that pain, and those ice-packs and punctures and clipped-shut swollen seams, and I glance up, outside, to see strolling past the coffee place what looks like my boyfriend, I'm sure it is, I think, holding hands with someone, both of them slipping their tongues around ice cream cones in per-fect and blithe sync. I can't tell if it's a grown-up-looking little girl or a girlish, well-held-together mature woman. I can't tell if it's a mother or a daughter, or either, and does it even matter, I realize I don't know which story to believe, which is more real or more made up. Maybe no one was ever in pain or thrall. I just see the hand-holding, and the stroll, and my insides are all going to spill, like I've been gutted, split open, then left alone on a hook to hang.

I look down and see I've stapled a finger, clean through the very tip, where it's all nerve and just a very little flesh, no blood, really. Driven through and punched tight, and it feels like absolutely nothing at all. Surprising, that it feels like nothing. I would have thought it would feel completely like something else.

DADDY?

It's late and my father's bedroom light is out. But I knock, anyway. I was thinking that just maybe he'd be waiting up, that he'd grill me about where I was or who I was with. I can't remember the last time he did that. I can't remember the last time he questioned me as he used to, the last time he was worried or strict, the last time he braided my hair or bathed me, told me I was pretty or wonderful or smart, dressed me, came into my room at night, sweet, undressed me, punished me, cared. The special kind of father things.

There's no answer, but I open the door and go in, anyway.

NEEDLES

They're in Needles for the night. At least, that was the plan.
But Rick had shut his phone off against her early in the day's
white glare and she'd lost sight of the weaving truck after his
angry, game-play cutoff on the westbound I-40, just past the
Arizona border. Day's end she spotted the heat-rippled Needles
off-ramp and the Motel 6 sign. Worth a try. She has her panting, paw-sweat little dog with her, and all Motel 6's take little
dogs—it's been their chain of choice the last three nights since
leaving Des Moines. Her driving her car in front, hands clenched
at 10 and 2, Rick coasting along back of her in the rental truck,
with a diminishing cooler of beer and a year's worth of her accu-
mulated thrift store crap she just couldn't bring herself to leave
behind this time, homeward bound, heading west, convoy ho.
She's sick of baking macadam, and pink-furred roadkill bounced

to the shoulder, and Christian radio static. She's sick of strategy and bluff. No truck in the Motel 6 parking lot, but she doesn't care, she's stopping for the night.

But yeah, he's checked in, as planned. She tells the grave-yard-shift teenager behind the counter, a girl with flayed hair and eyelined, won't-ever-make-it-further-into-California-than-this eyes, that she's his girlfriend. The girl shrugs, slaps on the counter a second key ringed on a red plastic diamond. It's after nine at night and there's still burning air going, still blaze and blistering skin.

The window AC in Room 117 is gasping out chill. No actual Rick, but his backpack is flung on one of the twin beds. On the nightstand, a bucket of soggy ice and a motel tumbler with gath-ered ocher drops. Beer for the road, bourbon at rest stops. The usual game. She's known this for twelve years and still begged him out to Iowa at the end of her visiting professor term to help get her moved back home again, or just moved back, just get her moved. He'd listened to the usual conditions, and still promised, agreed. They know the rules printed inside the cardboard lid by heart by now. She fills her little dog's water bowl from the tap, throws in a few ice cubes, and the dog laps and laps. She's tempted to cool-shower rinse, grab a patty melt at the Denny's next door, get into a rough-sheeted twin bed and sleep. But there is still the token move. She gives her little dog yesterday's sweat-stiff T-shirt to bunk into, and a kiss, a stomach rub, and heads out.

She hunts the four-street grid of Needles, finds the truck parked crooked and blocking a trailer's driveway on the last gravel road before desert scrub. A loose pyramid of fist-smashed beer cans on the passenger seat, her moving boxes stuffed tight and pressed rhomboid in the bed. There are three bars on this block, and she picks the saddest postcard one, with Xmas lights still looped above the faux-adobe entrance, unlit. The air inside is damp, sour saloon air, and he's at the far end of the bar, gulping from a tumbler and nodding passionately at an old soaked-and-smoked man with shaky cracked hands, mumbling into an old man's clutched glass. She gets up close behind him and she knows he knows she's there without turning around.

Get out of here, he says. I'm busy. I love this guy.

Let's get some sleep, Rick.

I quit. I'm out. I'm hitting the road. Be in L.A. by morning. You get your stuff later somewhere.

Come on, she says.

You have to listen to him. You have to love this guy. You have to.

I can't, she says. You know that.

She touches his bare elbow, below his sleeve, but he both jerks away and shoves at her.

I'm not playing anymore, he says. You can't do this to me, like always, like you do.

If he lurches out, she decides while he rants, if he makes it into the truck, drives off with all her worldly crap in the world onto black lost desert roads, she's calling the highway patrol. That's the next move. The new plan. When he begins to cry like he does she gets him off his stool, gets him under an arm and out the door and into her car, glad it's finally gone dark and moon-glow cool. He's crying, all shakes and bourbon sweat. She gets him back to the icy Motel 6 room, gets him onto one of the twin beds. She locks the chain lock, flops on the other bed next to her sleep-shivering little dog.

I'm so disgusting, he says. I'm so sorry.

I'm sorry, too, she says. For all of it.

He cries and cries, until she goes to him. She edges onto the cliff of nylon comforter, rubs his arm, gives him a pat on the head like a pet, but not like a dog. He grips her T-shirt hem.

Please lie here with me, he says, his voice cracking. That's all, I promise. Just lie.

She moves, lies carefully on her side in front of him. He curls behind her, sour mouth gulping at her hair, arm locked around her ribs, like they do.

This is all I ever wanted from you, he cries. All I want, I swear. Why can't I have just this?

APOLOGY

He comes home for dinner three hours late, but at least he's come home. It's a good sign, she's sure. A sign of healing, the first delicate crust of a scab. She's made a meal of his favorites from long ago, from when she was good and attentive to that kind of thing—a real meal, one that demanded hours of preparation and produced a cruel steam burn on her wrist. A meal of remorse.

Honey, just sometimes? he'd pleaded to her months ago, jabbing at the Styrofoam, *You're a great cook, can't we have a real dinner, not takeout, just once?*

And just once can't you open a fucking can? she'd bitched back, impatient and frayed.

Now she wishes she'd chewed off her tongue, met him halfway. Now, all ready for him: veal roast carved into limp petals, lobster risotto with saffron, asparagus with hollandaise, all served on the wedding crystal and china and silverware they've rarely ever used. A pear tart with fresh pears, and a from-scratch graham cracker crust. A meal made with much care.

Forgive me, all the food says.

She's tried to keep the tart warm without drying it out. She's tried to keep the sauces fresh with hourly infusions of butter and Marsala wine, tried to keep tamped down the impatience and fray. By the time he comes home, late, but at least he's come home, it's a good sign, she's put Esther and Justin to bed over protests; it will be just the two of them at this dinner, him and her at the dining room table with vanilla votives lit, the first time in a long time. He's come back, he's home, so what if he's late? This special, shared, intimate meal: Now they'll be able to move on, heal. But instead of eating her dinner when he arrives, he just stands there a moment, not meeting her eyes and dumping his duffel bag on the freshly waxed entryway floor, and she can see pressed into his face the memory of the last time he came home, six days ago, came home early from work, three or four hours earlier than usual, earlier than he was supposed to, when he stood in the entryway hearing, first, the silence of the house, then, hearing. *My house, in my house!* he'd wailed, like wronged husbands in noir or camp, and he was right, she knew, although *It's my house, too!* she'd wanted to assert back, even then, but didn't. The kids at school and daycare, and she, his wife, supposed to be at work, and yet there was something to hear. He glowers now, he walks down the hall and away from her, she hears him pause at what would be the door to their bedroom, then he passes it, goes straight into the kids' room, wakes them up to say hello, to let them know he's come home. She hears crying, all of them wracked. He's three hours late because he's shattered, crippled, rent, all her fault, truly, and her heart goes out to him now, literally; she can see her heart cracking through her chest and hurtling toward him in dripping, contrite offering. Her sauces have congealed, but it's all her fault, really, and at least he's home. He has spent six days and five nights at his cousin Don's, whom he cannot stand but was better than her, until the phone calls from Esther brought him back. Their little girl getting hysterical on the phone, pleading with him to come home, not understanding. *I know you did something bad, Mommy,* she said to her mother every day he was gone. She looked at her mother with an accusatory scowl, with his face, she's such his child, but was too scared to really let her have it; she sensed, primally, her mother might be all she had left. *You did something bad and that's why Daddy isn't here.*

She knows he will stay with the kids until they fall back into reassured, open-mouthed, hiccupping sleep. Presents for them in his pockets, probably, candy or stickers or temporary tattoos, he'll tease them and soothe. But his return won't absolve her, in their eyes; he has come home a weeping open wound. He wants them to see him bleed. Now, he'll turn them against her. She cleans up the kitchen, the offered and unaccepted food, and imagines with guilt the baby calf, force-fattened and cramped into a box, the live lobster thrust in boiling water, both of them dying for this showy display of contrition she'd tried to make, all for nothing.

She puts away the crystal, the china, because he hates it when she leaves things dirty or lying around, scratches the dead, smoky votives free of clinging wax and puts them to soak, polishes the sterling flatware by hand, accidentally slices a fingertip replacing the carving knife in its box, and when she comes into the living room she finds him on the living room couch, asleep, fully dressed and curled into an anguished fetal ball. He has made up a bed for himself with Esther's little girl-sized *Beauty and the Beast* sheets, a scratchy sofa pillow under his head. She, as she has done for the last five nights, goes to sleep in their double bed, alone. She puts her fingertip with its tiny, trifling cut in her mouth, sucks. She curls onto her side, presses her knees together, feels her naked thighs feel each other, hard. It hits her in full. She's soiled it, their house, their bedroom, their bed. She knows he's still seeing her naked at two in the afternoon, their flowered bedsheets grabbed to her breast and her most extravagant lace bra and panties on the floor. He still hears the voice behind him from the dark loom of their walk-in closet, such nice closets this house has, a selling point for them six years ago, her pregnant with Esther and both of them so interested in cabinetry, termite inspections, the condition of carpet pile. She still hears that voice, too, male, nervous, stupid—*Hey, man, you caught us, I'm sorry, man,* a sheepish huff of laughter—and thinks, What was I doing, what was I thinking? Wrapped in the cheap percale sheets he'd always hated but she'd insisted on buying—*Honey, can't you make the bed in the mornings, how long does that take, really*? he'd complained, *Hey, I have to be at work earlier than you do,* she'd carped right back, *You make the damn bed*—two ugly sets for the price of one. She'd been trying to save money, she wanted to have another baby, have four of them together in this magazine house, symmetrical and sheltered. But now she knows he still smells it in this house, in their bed. The acidic, musky leak of what she's done. The stain it's left. He can't be expected to forgive because of a silly pear tart and lobster risotto. He can't be expected to ever breathe that taint in again, of course not. What was she thinking, pinning hope on that one take-it-all-back meal, that one weak try at cleansing, restoring, that one sad chalkboard sweep?

She gets up early to make him breakfast, another thing she'd let go of doing but it'll be easier now that she's going to quit her job, won't be working anymore, and finds the Beast wrapped around his neck, Beauty in a kicked-off crumple at his feet.

No one could ever love you as much as I do, he'd said when he proposed, the sweetest, purest vow she'd ever heard, a happy promise, all that love.

WHEN HE COMES home a few nights later, he sniffs at the scent of blister and singe. He doesn't look at her, just around the house, sniffing, a question on his face. She opens the sliding glass door with a sort of bow and he follows her out to the backyard, where she shows him the barbecue pit's fluttery, charred mound: two flowered, percale double-sized sets, fitted and flat, pillow-slips, matching comforter, all now blackened with flame or drifted away as smoke. She shows him around the side of the house, near the trash cans: the maple bed frame, the mattress and box spring, all disassembled and dragged outside on her back, now waiting for Goodwill. She's purified the tainted air. She's cleansed the soul of the house. He kicks at the barbecue pit heap; ashes float, something cracks. He follows her back into the house, then, yes, into their bedroom, where he stops this time at the sight of new-ness, the alkaline smell of laundry detergent and carpet deodor-ant and lemon-oiled wood. A new oak bedroom set, a California king mattress this time, new pima cotton sheets and duvet with fresh sateen comforter, everything unused, unslept in, unsoiled.

You will be the only man who will ever lie in this bed, it all announces, *Please.*

They get into the new bed that night, the sheets' uncrushed fibers scraping their elbows. They get in wearing long T-shirts and underwear, but they get in together. They get in together, but on opposite sides of its wide, crisp, California-king expanse, and they stay there, a gutter of space still between them. He is turned protectively away from her, like children are taught in grade school to curve away from bomb-blasted windows, from flying and dangerous debris. Protect your vulnerable organs, your face. But she wants to touch him; she wants him to touch her. She wants him pressing her knees apart, her thighs. She slides her hand across the bed toward him, she sees his shoulders cringe away, and she stops. He might succumb to the pressure of new sheets, yes, he might lay himself on those virgin sheets free of sweat, hairs, flakes of skin, but no, he won't bear even the slightest touch of her hand. New sheets, bed, what a ludicrous, superficial try. Every inch of her skin, she understands now, finally, is stained with someone else's breath, tongue, come—*You're a bitch, you know that?* he'd yelled, throwing shirts and slacks in the duffel bag, *The mother of my kids, you didn't think about that?*—and she wonders how to burn the reek of that away, sear from her every dirty layer, cell, molecule ever possessed by someone else. She can't, and it takes seven years for a body to regenerate itself, cell by cell, marrow and organs and bone; can she live this way for seven years, her children lured away from her—*They're my kids, too*, she'd thought back then, in protest, thinks even now—and every night having to face the thickening fence of her husband's back, until she's clean and new again? If she has to, she will, but he can't. He doesn't deserve that, any of this, he doesn't deserve a used, handled, loaned-out wife. A wife she made common—*fucking bitch*, *slut*—public.

No one could ever love you as much as I do, it's still true now, she knows, despite what she's done and although they're sharing the house, the bed, like strangers. It will always be true; he will always be true. So what was she doing, what made her do it, and how does she show him she believes him, that she knows he's right, and that she's still, forever, his?

SHE WEARS ONLY a nightshirt a few weeks later, one of his, an old-fashioned pajamas' top cut like a man's shirt, soft checked flannel, with a pocket and three buttons down the front. Her drawerfuls of lingerie, all that fancy lace, won't do right now. It didn't take a holiday or special occasion; he'd come home once or twice a month with small bow'd boxes and tissue-stuffed gift bags crammed with lace, frills, gauze, pricey little wisps for her to wear. She'd model for him, walk around the house like that, *No one will ever love you, this body, all of this body as much as I do*, he'd say, his eyebrows making it a mock-threat, putting his hands, his mouth, on her breasts, pushing fingers between her legs, until Esther was maybe twelve or eighteen months old, then she'd just wear those things underneath her clothes, give him a flash in the morning as she left for work. But after Justin was born, two years ago, she had trouble losing the weight. She'd always been full-breasted, full-hipped, *Voluptuous*, he used to say, making chomping noises, but after having Esther and then Justin, it was hard. Her flesh looked awful, she thought, clumsy and bulging against net fabrics and elastics and lacy strings—*Honey, you're so beautiful, what about those diet shakes, what about aerobics?* he'd suggest oh so helpfully—and all that lingerie, forget it, she could barely squeeze into her old suits for work. She tried, but nothing she tried had any effect. *What about getting up early to go running?*

Then, *Michael, you have to meet the real power here, she's who really runs the place,* Nancy had said, leading over the new guy, the new operations manager, who shook hands pleasantly and laughed at her embarrassed retort to Nancy and later that week saw her drinking peppermint tea, day after day—*Honey, what about that cabbage diet, what about fasting once a week?*—all day with no lunch, and so a few weeks later brought her a Lipton's Herbal Mint Sampler, who two months later invited her for a cheesy afternoon high tea at the Hilton to discuss accounts and blinked, bewildered, when she refused cake, then ordered her a bowl of fresh berries instead and fed her the first one, spread with clotted cream, by hand. She remembers touching her throat and neck, confused, ruffled, and suddenly feeling the strap of her bra, still wearing a maternity bra then, although Justin was two, the huge cotton cups the only kind that felt like support. This new guy, this Michael, this now faceless and arbitrary person, smiled, and she remembers hoping he wouldn't see the strap, and then hoping that he would. And she remembers remembering those drawerfuls of abandoned lace, the feeling of blood rushing to a hot swell.

But she can't wear any of it now, maybe ever again, not after he saw it on the floor, *his* lingerie, *his* peach lace bra and panties on the floor. She knows he still sees it. And it still hurts. It hurts both of them, still. She can't even wear a bra right now, not since she had it done. She gets into bed wearing his nightshirt, and this time she does reach over to him, she reaches determinedly for his hand. For the first time, he lets her. She tugs, and he rolls over toward her, but not meeting her eyes. She puts his hand on her neck, her throat, she wants him to reclaim her. She wants his weight pinning her, flattening her out. His fingers tighten a moment on her throat and then stroke. She unbuttons the three buttons of the flannel pajamas' top and brings his hand down to her breast, her left breast, it's still sore but the itching has stopped, the slight scabbing has worn away.

Look, she says to him, but he shakes his head, this is agony for him, and he closes his eyes. The needles had hurt most around her nipple and over her breastbone, her collarbone, the thicker needle for the outline a deeper, sharper pierce, the finer needles for shading like a ruthless scratching of cats' claws, like relentless bee stings. A good hurt, a willing, penitent hurt. *Please, look*, she implores. He opens his eyes and sees what she's done: his name, thick, black, cursive, etched wide across her thorax, her left breast engraved with a scarlet heart. A seal, a label, a brand, she'll wear it forever, *I'm all yours, forever*, it pleads. He covers his scripted name with his hand, his face warps; he presses his mouth against her throat and starts to cry. She kisses the top of his shaking hair. *Believe me*. His grip on her breast grows tighter, distorting the scrawl. He cries, and she cries, too, grateful, thankful that he's crying like one of her babies she can comfort, do for, make everything right for, finally, then he takes her nipple in his mouth with a hard suck, a bite. She's grateful for that, too, remembering the needle there, the black ink stabbed into the thin rosy skin of the areola, but then he bites harder, beyond bruise, beyond show, grinding his teeth on her flesh. He's going for blood, she realizes, and she cries out for him to stop.

He does, he shoves her away, and she closes her eyes in failure. And shame, that she couldn't take it, couldn't begin to bear what he has had to. She hears him leave their bed. She hears the faucet blast violently in the bathroom, hears the splash of water and the slick, lathery rub of soap.

INTERESTING, WHAT HURTS and what doesn't. Piercing the fleshy lobe of your ear is a dull crunch, there are no nerves there, really, no blood, no pain, or you misinterpret the sudden needle punch as pain when it's really just something abrupt. Esther wants to get her ears pierced like her mother's, but she's told her she can't until she's thirteen. Esther hates her for that now, too. Five years old, and she's lost the right to be her mother. Esther knows that, she wields it, and she's right. She's glad Justin is still too young, too innocent, to really understand. Maybe there's still a chance for them, a chance for her little boy's unadulterated love.

Ice helps. She bleeds, she swells, but the ice pack, clutched clumsily as she makes her way to the car afterward, numbs her out. It didn't, doesn't really hurt. Not like the hurt she's caused him. Not like the hurt of knowing how what she's done to him hurts.

Feel, she says to him a few weeks later. *Here, feel*. His back is to her, still, always, but the curve of it is less tight, as if his exhausted spine and muscles can no longer sustain such rigid guard. She slides her whole body toward him, carefully, and presses up behind. His hand is lying on his thigh, unclenched, the fingers limp as a child's. The fingers tremble a bit. She puts her hands on his shoulder and gently tips him onto his back. He lets her. She lies carefully on top of him, careful not to crush, her head in the pillow above his shoulder so he doesn't have to see her face, and after long, tense-relax, tense-relax moments, she feels his arms steal around her body, a hand caress her hair, his fingers pressing into her waist. She takes his hand, carefully places it between her legs.

Here, feel, she says. She feels before he does, though, she feels his fingers clutch at the heat, the damp, the hair, then stop. She feels the jolt in her nerves, and then she feels the confusion in his hand. His fingers fumble with the two tiny rings in her swollen flesh, the cold surgical steel chain. The links clink. A tiny metal lock, too, in the shape of a heart, like you'd find on a young girl's diary, the kind that opens with a tiny medieval-looking key. She hands him the key.

No other man will ever touch me again, it vows.

She rolls onto her back and draws her legs apart. There are tremors all through him, but he's growing hard; he grasps the key tight, determined, his eyes narrowed on it, and unlocks the tiny locked heart that seals her closed, unthreads the chain from the rings, and spreads her wide. He sits back on his knees, pulls her toward him from under her hips, his eyes still focused there, and enters her abruptly, good, an abrupt and tearing drive. She's waited until she was mostly healed but not all healed, because she doesn't have the right to be all healed before he is. Then, he does it harder.

You're a whore, you know that? he says, moaning. *You're just a fucking whore to me now.*

She hears a padded shuffle in the thick carpet pile outside their bedroom door, a hiccup, Justin's sweet baby hiccup— *Whore, cunt*, he says, louder, and a crueler plunge—and she cringes at her little boy on the other side of their door, needing her and hearing this. She cringes, and then she hears a soft, hesitant pad of retreat. It's too late, there's nothing she can do but stay where she is, wide open, apart, and flat. Each deeper thrust he makes is both a splitting and a pact. She arches and spreads wider for him, the only way to show him she's his, all his, that she's willing to sacrifice. To exist with him wholly in a slick open pain, to become all wound.

No one will ever love you as much as I did, he groans, and now, she realizes, it is a curse.

THEY WERE GIVEN service for twelve: the Rosenthal china ("Eden" pattern: dinner, salad, bread and butter, coupe soup) and Baccarat crystal (wine goblet, champagne flute, tumbler) she'd cut from a magazine. She chooses a flute, sets it at a place for one. An ivory lace cloth on the dining room table, and the kids, his kids, gone to bed without protest, a brief hug from Justin, a cold, resigned peck from Esther. This is how it is now, how it will always be, as long as she lives in this house, his house. She sits, takes a deep breath, admires the silverwork on the polished handle of the sterling knife, steadies herself, then cuts with much care. She slowly fills the flute, and the crystal turns warm in her hand.

He comes home late, just as she expected, because she understands now that he will always come home late. But he will always come home.

She offers the glass to him with a shaky hand.

Is this what you want? she asks. Will this finally do it?

He takes the glass from her, looks at it; in the fading light its contents glow a thick, sanguine red. She feels her very marrow has begun, at last, not to regenerate but to seethe. Too late. She's shaking, she's limp and drained.

Will this be my life now? she asks. Will it?

Yes, he says, looking her dead in the eye. He raises the glass.

I'm sorry, he says, and drinks.

FISH

She is in town to dispose of her uncle, but she can't do that until he dies. It is Any Time Now. She is eyeing the creeping analog clock hands on any wall, the digital display outside every savings and loan. She is tapping her foot, drumming fingers, chomping at the bit. And, she is organized: The local Neptune Society phone number is entered in her always-charged phone; the power of attorney document is in her date-book and the DNR form is on file, for if and when there's any ugly hospital debate over invasive procedures or more tubes; she has gone to his dingy studio apartment, in a seniors' complex smelling of Pine-Sol and fish bones and flakes of skin, selected his final clothes, and has them in a plastic grocery bag in the trunk of her rental car. Jeans and once-white cotton Henley, the kind she remembers him wearing when she was a child, gone now to a stale ivory. She figured that was the best choice, natural, biodegradable fibers. The Neptune Society had not offered explicit instructions on this, but she imagined polyester or rayon or viscose wouldn't burn well. She had a terror of getting a call that a bad melt of synthetic fibers had ruined the crematory slab or emitted a toxic gas. She was concerned she'd get billed for it. That there would be a protracted legal dispute, all of it angry and ultimately pointless. She wonders why the body needs to be dressed at all—let's just unhook the monitors and IV, strip the gown away, wheel it off to the oven. She pictures her uncle's doughy naked body splayed on a big, wooden pizza paddle, a burly Neapolitan man giving it a quick jerk of a shove into flames. Afterward, the Neptune Society will throw the cremains in a body of water for her, if she wishes— the Mississippi, she assumes—or hand them over to dispose of herself. They're sensitive to the family's preference. She doesn't want them. What would she do with them? Does anyone in real life keep ashes on the mantel, in an urn? She's not buying an urn. She wishes the river, by all means. Let the ashes float like a tap of fish food, let the bone fragments and Levi's rivets sink down to the silt. She will have him ready to go. That's her job. She has already boxed up his meager belongings, has glanced at then thrown away the album'd and carefully framed family photos he'd kept all these years—everyone in outdated clothing and hairstyles, posing together with camera-false smiles—and donated the rest to Goodwill. She'd hesitated over the long-unused fishing rod and tackle, the hat with its dangling hooks, wondering if they might fetch a good eBay price, then tossed all of that in, too, not wanting anything prolonged. She's already written *deceased* on a copy of his lease and sent it to the complex manager; it's premature, but he certainly won't be going back there. Which she's glad of, it's a blessing, no more need to imagine him banished to a lonely beige box of a room, watching an endless loop of cop-and-game-show TV, eating salmon from an individual serving can and munching on saltines from the pack. She'll write *deceased* on his final round of bills, on any junk mail, on the stub she'll send back from his final Social Security check. Which ought to cover the cost of the Neptune Society. She estimates, thanks to her organization, that roughly one more total hour of her time, no more, will be spent on all of this once he's dead. She imagines herself getting a stopwatch, going *click* with it at the final rattle of his final breath, saying *Go!*, and timing it down to the second. She is not the true, technical next of kin—there is still her mother, the uncle's blood sister, and her two own older siblings—she is merely the one who assumes this kind of job, the one everyone assumes will do it. And she is the one her uncle had chosen; it is her name, in what she assumes was a moment of perverse nostalgia, or punishment, or trust, that he had written on forms. No, no one will question her account of events this time, or get in the way. The family's wishes are all hers to wish. She is happy to fulfill this obligation, to be the one in charge of closure. She is pawing at the ground, chewing her nails, twisting her hair. If she smoked, she'd be constantly lighting up, one eye squinting at the clock through a nostriled plume.

For now, she is sitting in chain restaurants with photos of food on their laminated menus, reading used pulp mysteries bought for twenty-five cents off a cart in the hospital lobby. She is sucking relentlessly on small hard candies she keeps in her pockets, leaving their crumpled cellophanes behind wherever she goes. She is going to matinees, for the discount admission and chunk of time it kills. She is checking her office voice-mail, e-mailing updates with brief declarative sentences to her parents. She is seeing the sights: the Arch, the plane that Lindbergh flew, the world-famous Botanical Garden. She goes to a riverboat casino that calls Twain to mind, methodically inserts twenty dollars' worth of quarters in a slot machine, and leaves without winning or losing another cent. She is eating frozen custard, which people here seem to eat a lot of, even as the weather is turning chill. People in the Midwest in general seem very large to her. She wonders how the local Neptune Society deals with this. If all that fat makes it harder to do their job. Her uncle has gotten fatter, too, in the dozen plus years since she saw him last, waving good-bye to her from his car, his fishing hat askew, although he seems shrunken at the same time; she remembers him as jolly-fat, energetic, always proposing to the child her some fun game they could play together, some special adventure they could go off on, just the two of them, alone. She hopes the guy with the pizza slide won't have a problem getting him to burn. She knows no one in St. Louis except, of course, her uncle and, now, the doctors and nurses. She goes to the hospital for fifteen minutes in the morning and fifteen minutes in the evening to check on How He's Doing. It is Any Time Now, they tell her. It is A Waiting Game. She is called upon to do nothing; there are tubes going in and tubes going out, the pillows and sheets are arranged, and the meds, now, keeping pain managed, organs running hydrated and calm. She sits in a chair in the corner of his room, listens to his shallow breathing, to the beeps and faint hospital-speak PA announcements, and reads until the next quarter hour. Sometimes she brings chocolates or little hard candies to the doctors and nurses. They're sure he knows she's there, they tell her, despite his incomprehensive gaze and his incomprehensible mumbles. She's relieved he is incapable of actual speech. The nurses tell her he is lucky to have such a wonderful niece. They asked, when she first arrived, if there were other family members they should contact.

No, she told them. We have no other family. It's just the two of us.

She makes very sure, each time she leaves, that they have her cell number.

SHE LIKES THE Botanical Garden. There's an Orchid House, and a section devoted to mutant roses, and a lily pond with enormous flat fronds the pamphlet tells her native women used to let their babies sleep upon while they pounded clothes clean. There's a Shakespeare Garden, with multiple references to Ophelia. There's a Japanese section, with bonsai and small beds of pebbled sand raked into rows to evoke Zen. She takes deep breaths as she strolls here; this place should bring peace of mind, without asking, like flight attendants bring the beverage service at twenty minutes in. A diminutive river flows along, a clear green swath. *There are a dozen varieties of koi, here at the Missouri Botanical Garden,* the pamphlet tells her. She'd like to see them and their dozen varieties, but there is always a throng of tourists clogging the red wooden footbridge, usually couples and families with small children, and they're always very loudly engaged by the fish, laughing and pointing as they throw food. The children jump up and down. It's now her third trip to the Botanical Garden, and she's increasingly annoyed by this agitation. The Japanese section would be very peaceful, if it weren't for all the squealing and fish-pointing. The camera-clacking. She can't remember her family ever taking little sight- or fish-seeing excursions like this. Perhaps when she was very small. She tries to recall. All those smiley photos her uncle had taken and kept, yes, the outings as a family group. But she more readily pictures the moments left unshot, unsnapped. Her sister's attention-demanding tantrums in shopping malls and amuse-ment parks that provoked their parents to hurried exits, with-out anyone getting the promised roller-coaster ride or the art supplies needed for school. She thinks of her brother's inevita-ble asthma attacks and inconsistent food allergies, the relent-less parental attention to air quality and the ingredients of his meals, the usual vomiting of popcorn or jelly bellies or carrot sticks wherever they went. She remembers cleaning up his color-ful vomit. All the turmoil and fuss. This time, she decides, she will claim the bridge for herself. She wants to feed the fish, too. It is her right, after paying her Botanical Garden admission fee. Feeding the fish, quietly, will bring the peace, will be the Zen thing to do.

She waits for the crowd to move off in their two- and three- and foursomes, which takes a very long time. She resolves to wait it out. She paces a side path by herself, she taps her foot. She reads about the *beauty and tranquillity of koi* in the pamphlet. She coughs loudly. She buys, to be at the ready, a quarter's worth of fish food from the small gumball-looking machine: a handful of grainy brown crumbles, suspiciously fish-scented. She won-ders if the Botanical Garden grind their dead fish into fish food. She wonders if this causes mad cow disease among koi. *Under the right conditions, koi have a possible lifespan of one hundred years!* the pamphlet tells her. Unlikely, then, that they're forced to feed on their dead own.

The last of the crowd is finally gone, and she eagerly approaches the bridge. The little green river has rippled out to glass. The food sticks to her palm, and she imagines a scattering of flakes from her gentle, Lady Bountiful hand, the grateful fish swimming near with beauty and tranquillity, taking nourishment from her, then swimming off and away with content grace. But the moment her foot hits red wood there's a wet flapping, a swell. The water turns orange and yellow, turns spotted black and white, turns garish, comes alive with writhe. She steps up fully on the bridge and looks down; there are a dozen of them, more, rushing the water at a stress, cramming together and up at her. They are large fish, the size of dachshunds. They cram together in a thrashing mass. It's horribly untranquil, unbeautiful. Their black eyes are fierce. Their open mouths are stretched open hard, surging, breaking the surface by inches. If fish could scream, there would be screams. She remembers a gaping, pulsing mouth like that. She remembers a sharp hook pierced clean through, off fishing with her uncle that time, the two of them, the celebration of her first silvery-in-the-air catch flashing to horror, becoming a cold little fish caught by its hooked mouth, screaming, the special treat of a day at the lake turned ugly and twisting and wet in her hand.

She opens her fist; the brown crumbles drop down into throats but the lurching mouth rings don't stop. A glowing red fish with yellow-ring'd black eyes leaps up, angry. There's an insidious turmoil from the rest. She swipes the last of the food from her sweaty hand and stumbles backwardly off the bridge. She turns to run when she hits the regular footpath, bordered by smooth stones and beds of combed sand.

HE IS HANGING On, the desk nurse tells her. Probably for you.

She doesn't know how to respond to this. It feels like both tribute and blame.

You can tell him it's okay, a nurse's aide tells her, quietly, when they are alone with her uncle. Let him know he doesn't have to hang on for you. You can tell him he can let go.

But that never works, she thinks.

She pats her uncle's hand, the one uncomplicated by an IV. It is dry, liver-spotted, the ridged nails extending just beyond the spatulate tips. His eyes flicker open at her touch, the lids then droop closed. One doctor has told her it's mere reflex, this reaction; a nurse has insisted he sees her, logs her in, that her familial presence is oxygenating or strength-maintaining, the thing that inspires his heroic endurance. Even if he does see her, she wonders, would he know her? And what would he say to her, now?

The nurse's aide is combing her uncle's strands of hair into neat rows across his scalp. They do a nice job of keeping him tidy, she has noticed. They talk about dignity. A dignified, peaceful end, that's what they promise. In kind, sepulchral tones. No discussion of actual timeframe, though, no guarantees there.

Would you like to do this? the nurse's aide asks, offering an instrument. It is a pair of nail clippers, shiny and mean. Sometimes the family likes to do this kind of thing, he tells her, Sometimes it's comforting. If you want to.

She takes the nail clippers from him. It seems undignified to manicure herself right now, here. No, she realizes. This is so I can tend to him. Do it to him, for him. She takes a deep breath, tries not to look at the clock on the wall. She tries not to look horrified. She picks up her uncle's hand, the one she already patted, had finished with. This is not her job.

Let go, she wishes. *Let go, let go. Go.*

But the aide, dissatisfied with the tidiness of the first parting, is still arranging her uncle's rust-and-gray hair, carefully raking new rows. Humming an indistinguishable tune under his breath while not leaving. A bulge in his mouth shifts cheeks, and she realizes he is sucking on one of her hard candies. He has that swollen midwestern look, skin shiny and pink and stretched taut, the aspect of a ceramic piggy bank. She feels people in the health industry should not allow themselves to grow to such proportions. They are in a position of authority; they should set a healthy, positive example. Her uncle, while withering, is still huge to her, like when she was little. She

pictures him in the oven, skewered, his fat bubbling then dripping to a sizzle. She starts with his thumb, his large, unfrail
thumb. She takes it in her fist and feels how the skin is loose
now around the bone. She remembers his powerful hands on
her shoulders. She remembers his hands thrusting a wet bait
worm onto a hook. Beeps from the heart machine above her
uncle's head accelerate; she watches the little neon spikes mul-
tiply briefly across the screen, then slow to normal. Is this a
reflex? she wonders. A body's natural response to stimuli? Or
does he know it's her, does he recognize the familiar, familial
feel of her hand? She grips him harder, to hold the thumb shaft
steady, and catches the edge of dry yellow nail in the clipper's
jaws. She hesitates, tells herself it's just a ridge of dried protein,
a bit of human glut, it is nothing to fear. She tells herself this
is the least she can do. Her mouth is dry; she wishes for a sweet
hard candy in her mouth.

I don't want to hurt him, she murmurs to the aide. Really.

Oh, you won't, the aide assures. Besides, his voice drops to
discreet, wafts butterscotch at her, He is so doped up anyway.
You just go on. It's a nice thing to do. He steps back, admiring his
own work. He adjusts a reddish hair. The humming begins again,
as if a small insect has flown into the room.

She snips at the excess nail, careful not to cut skin, working her way across. The nail is tough; the clipper squeezing takes
more force than she would have thought, and it grows slippery in

her sweating hand. She tries to swallow. A jagged yellow moon of nail finally drops to the white sheet.

There you go! the aide encourages, That's it. He puts the comb away in a wicker basket of toiletries. He wipes a bit of moisture from her uncle's loose mouth with a tissue, tosses it in the wastebin by the sink.

I like to involve the family, he says. I think it brings a good feeling.

Yes, she says.

He washes his hands, gathers his things, his basket, adjusts the blood pressure cuff hanging in a wire bin attached to the wall. He tugs the plastic liner from the wastebin, hefts the small bag of trash. I'll be back! he announces cheerily as he leaves. The insect hum goes with him down the hall, grows fainter then gone.

She hurries to finish, finger, finger, finger. She pauses to wipe her hand on her sweater. It seems to be taking a long time, and her morning fifteen minutes are almost over. More clippings drop to the sheet. Almost done. She doesn't want the aide to return to find she didn't finish her job; she doesn't want to be there when he returns. What's next, Q-tips to swab his ears, wipe crust from his eyes, a shave? Ointment on weeping bedsores? No, she isn't going to be hooked in like that. She pushes toward the end, her hand aching. The last clipping falls; the sheet is littered with them. She puts the instrument down on the Formica table arm that swings across the bed. She gathers up the hard, sharp moons in her sweaty palm; there is nowhere to leave them, the wastebin liner has not been replaced. She puts the clippings in her sweater pocket, next to a hard candy. She wants desperately to scrub her hands but doesn't want to be caught exhibiting such distaste. She hurries away, down the disinfected hospital hall, before she is spotted and asked to do anything else.

THERE IS NOTHING to fear, she tells herself. She heads along the path, toward the little red footbridge. The Garden is tranquil; it's the middle of a school day, a work day, and there is an audible lack of family or tourist noise. A discreet cricket or two, a muted breeze through a world-famous variety of trees, loosening their dying autumn leaves. The river wholly still, as if empty of life. It's just as she hoped this time. This is the experience she's come for. This serenity, this peace. She inserts a quarter in the almost-empty gumball machine, receives her pellets of food. There's a flicker in the river, perhaps a trick of current and algae and sungleam. Then, that's all. She exhales, steps upon the red wooden slats of the bridge. A tailfin flaps; by the time she is midway across the bridge a single fish has appeared, its black-and-white spotted fish skin clearly visible through the clear liquid green. A small koi, sweet, perhaps not fully grown. It raises its mouth to the surface, partly open, polite, a hopeful request without insistence or force. She drops a few pellets into the fish's mouth and watches it swim away, appeased. Then another mouth appears; another fish, this one marked in pretty lemon stripes, has surfaced without causing a ripple in the water, must have swum straight up from the murky below. The first fish returns, quietly, its mouth apologetic and grateful. *The beauty and tranquillity of koi,* how true. She decides to spend another quarter on another fistful of food. She steps back on the bridge and there, the flapping begins again, more and more fish now, the river is abruptly alive with their thrashing and foam, their garish colors mottling the green. Those appalling mouthtubes, thrusting out of the water at her. She shakes her hand over them, releasing the food straight down into gullets, but their frenzy grows. The large red one lunges up, its black, yellow-gleam eyes glaring. It remembers her, she is sure. She looks around for help—where are the families, the tourists? The food is all gone; she searches in her pockets for something, finds only an empty cellophane wrapper and hard bits of, what? She scoops the nail clippings up, mingled with bits of lint, leans, drops them into the red fish's mouth. She hopes the sharp sickles pierce holes in its fish insides, tear its guts apart. But its thrashing, its glaring at her goes on. Its appetite is livid, obscene, impossible to satisfy. She backs up and away, she flees the Garden. At least she can do that now, at least she has the power to run away.

THERE IS A new party line: This Could Take Awhile. His signs, the output of fluids, the cell counts, are not all merely holding steady, they are improving. He is a very strong man, they tell her. He could live to be a hundred, at this rate. She is furious, feels lured here by false promises. She is suddenly suspicious of the hospital staff; have they been conducting procedures behind her back? Deliberately prolonging this, putting heroic measures or artificial means into play the moment she leaves the room? Are they ignoring the family's wishes, misusing their authority? She cannot imagine staying here much longer; she has a life, after all. What will she do, she wonders, with his plastic bag of clothes? With his mail? Will he stay here, or will she have to find him a nursing facility? How much more will she have to do? To manage? To pay? And what if he becomes fully conscious again, becomes aware of her, regains the power of speech?

She thanks the morning nurse for the good news, says she'll be back that evening.

Her cell phone startles her. She is at the coffee shop next to the hospital, eating a club sandwich whose asymmetrical layers look nothing like the photograph on the menu. She is embarrassed by the loud ringtone but then notices other people on cell phones, locals talking in between large mouthfuls and swallows of their fatty food. Perhaps they are all playing the Waiting Game, too, on the phone with the doctors next door, getting updates on liver enzymes and biopsies and heart rates. Perhaps it's a mishap at work, a minor emergency she'll need to fly home and attend to at once. She answers her phone.

It's her mother. Again, she is startled. She has not spoken to her mother in over a year.

How is he? her mother wants to know. Are they taking good care of him, is there anything he needs?

She tells her mother her uncle is doing fine. Better than fine. Doing very well. He could live to be a hundred, at this rate. Under the right conditions.

Her mother does not ask what conditions those would be. Instead, she asks if he is in any pain.

She assures her mother he is in no discomfort at all. That all his needs are being tended to. Her mother can call the hospital herself, to check, if she wants. Really.

No, no, dear, that isn't necessary. Her mother is sure the doctors know what they're doing, that they are doing what's best.

Let go, let go, let go, she thinks.

Such a shame, her mother continues, Such a shame it all had to be this way. There's a pause, then: You aren't, you aren't bringing up any of that old fuss to the doctors, are you?

No, Mom. I am being a wonderful niece, she says. She sips coffee into her dry mouth. She feels again the conflicting yet familiar sense of both tribute and blame.

I'm sure you are, her mother says. But the voice sounds skeptical. Of course, her mother rarely believes her, or takes her side, about anything. She rarely ever has, in the end.

SHE RETURNS TO her uncle's hospital room to find the piggy nurse's aide giving him a trim, snipping the hairline clean above her uncle's baggy ears. The aide is in on it, he must be. They are trying to bring him back to life. There would be no need, otherwise, to keep her uncle so tidy and trim.

Well, you're back! the aide says. Weren't you already here this morning?

Yes, she says.

She watches the steady spikes on the monitor, listens to the regular beeps, tries to hear if his breathing has become stronger, more profound. She watches thin snips of hair fall to the pillow. She could gather those up, make a clump, tell the nurse's aide it's for a mourning locket, like in Victorian times. She could gather up more nail clippings. She could keep snipping away at him in the guise of care, cutting off bits of flesh here and there, calluses, moles, a polyp, those fleshy earlobes, work her way up to fingers and toes. Split his belly when no one is there to see, tug out a shiny organ or two. Cut out his fat tongue. Yes, perhaps the red fish would choke on that. Or perhaps it would be satisfied, at last, to have eaten its fill.

THE FOOD MACHINE has yet to be refilled. She wonders what on earth her Botanical Garden admission fees are being spent on. She should complain to someone. Make a fuss. Never mind. She is determined, wrapping her sweater around herself tight. She'll stand her ground, this time. Let it thrash. Let it scream those silent screams. It can't touch her. The Garden seems deserted. A few leaves float down. The little river is still. There's no disturbance when she steps up on the bridge. She waits a moment, then marches across to her spot. No sound, no uproar. She peers down into flat, immobile water, sees nothing. Stomps her foot. A leaf lands on the empty clear water, skates lazily along. It must be hiding. Lying in wait for her. Waiting to catch her alone like this, get her off-guard. She backs off the bridge, grabs a handful of pebbles from the nearest raked row. She throws a few pebbles into the water, causes minor ripples. She can see the pebbles sink clear to the river floor. She throws a few more, harder. Nothing. Are they sick? Have they died? She imagines tourist families fishing, angling for the fish, laughing as they bait and hook them, swinging them bleeding through the air, dumping them to choke and gasp on the bridge, gutting them, taking them away to a cornmeal dip and hot oil fry for Sunday dinner.

Winter.

She sees a man down the path, wearing a Botanical Garden uniform and carrying a rake, speaking at her. An open trash bag of dead leaves at his feet.

Excuse me? she says.

Winter's coming.

Yes, she says. You need to refill the food machine.

Not my job, he says. He drags a rake along the bed of sand she'd disturbed.

She resumes her watch of the water. They have to be there, she thinks. There has to be a way to get their attention, to lure.

No, winter they take the fish away, he tells her. No point waiting.

Oh.

River here's too shallow to keep them warm.

Where do they take them?

He shrugs. Safe place. Bring them back come spring.

His bed is smoothed into rows once again, every pebble in place. He moves on with his bag of leaves.

Somewhere protected, then, a safe, warm place. That's good. She wonders how they gathered up all those writhing fish. Someone with a net came, yes, balloon-scooped them along a slow sweep of water, lulling them, then carefully up to a safe and warm elsewhere. No hooks, of course. Not if the goal is bring them back whole come spring. Keep them alive, unhurt. She'd cried when her little fish was hooked, when she'd realized what she'd done. She'd made such a fuss. Other fishing men on the boat, laughing, paying no attention, ripping metal hooks from jaws or cutting through scaled white bellies with gleaming knives, dropping bright wet guts in bloody buckets, on deck. Other fish lying on planks, gaping mouths working against air, gills clenching then loose. And the little twisting rainbow fish in her cold hand, screaming. Her uncle suddenly there, *I'm here, don't be scared,* he'd said.

But it's screaming, she'd said, shaking. *It's screaming, help it, can't you hear?*

Let go, let go, taking the fish and showing her he could unhook the fish free, *It's okay, see?,* gently with his big fingers, snipping the line and working the cruel barb out with care, rinsing away thin blood to show her it was whole and good again. *See?* he'd said, holding her close and warming her as she gulped for air, *Everything's okay now.* He leaned over the edge of the boat, dropped the little fish home.

We don't have to fish anymore. We'll do something else. Whatever you want.

He'd wiped her teary cheeks, let her hiccup in his face, squeezed her hand in his massive fishy one. And they'd watched the fish swim away. She'd clutched on to his thumb.

Yes, something fun, he'd said, patting her. *Just the two of us.*

I'M SO SORRY, the nurse's aide tells her. We tried to get hold of you.

He places his plump hand on her arm without asking.

Excuse me? she says. She drops her sweater on the hallway floor, to have an excuse to pull away.

He passed on. About an hour ago. Very sudden. I am so sorry.

She hears the *Go!* click in her head. She can count final seconds now. The aide takes her to see him, again without asking. He is alone in a different room, small, chilled, in the basement. He is still in a regular hospital bed, not on a slab, lying under a neatly draped sheet that bulges across his belly. The tubes and monitors have been unhooked, are gone. There is the promised air of a dignified end.

Would you like to see his face?

She shakes her head. She is cold in this room, feels only numb.

I understand, the aide says. That's fine. Everyone deals in their own way.

Yes, she says. What happens now?

We'll need you to sign some forms. I'll go get them. Leave you two alone a moment.

Thank you, she says. Yes.

The aide pats her shoulder and she wills herself not to flinch. He walks off, his feet squeaking across the tiled floor.

Were you with him? she asks after him.

Oh, yes. Don't you worry, he wasn't alone.

That's good. I didn't want that. I never wanted that.

Of course not, the aide says.

I thought I should be here for him, you know? It was the least I could do.

Don't feel guilty, hon, you did everything you could. Don't you let that eat you up.

She nods, then asks:

Did he say anything?

The aide shakes his head. It was a very peaceful end, he says.

Good, she says.

Now she can feel it, the peace. She can call the Neptune Society, fill out the final date, use her rubber stamp, send all those forms off and away and be done with it. A peaceful end, yes. Nothing said. Nothing more to feel guilty about. She should remember to send the aide something, she thinks. A big box of chocolates or those hard candies, all for him, a special treat.

Anyone else you'd like me to call? the aide asks.

No. There's no other family. Just the two of us.

He nods, smiles understandingly, leaves.

She takes a handful of sheet, careful not to touch his bulk, and folds it down to reveal his dead rubber mask of a face. He is very still. His eyes and mouth are closed. She looks for a flicker, an eyelid's twitch. There's nothing. *Let go, let go,* she thinks. But she has to be sure. She moves aside the sheet, places two careful fingertips on the inside of his cooling wrist. Nothing. She watches the sheet resting over his chest, slowly counts

Mississippi seconds to one hundred, waiting for a rise and fall that doesn't come before she is convinced.

No, it's only almost over, she realizes. She isn't quite done yet.

THE LITTLE RIVER is scaled with crisp brown leaves. The Garden feels wintry, fully abandoned. She takes her place on the bridge and opens the plastic box: gritty bits and flakes, grays and blacks. She leans across the rail; there is no breeze and the ashes slide straight down into water, onto floating leaves, no comical blowing of puffs into face or hair as she's seen in movies. She takes a deep breath, fills her lungs with relief. She can go, let go. She breathes, and then she sees a blink of red. An autumn leaf, it must be. A wet red flash again, a surfacing ripple, leaves floating clear. A black eye gazing at her through water. The red fish is gliding, calm, watching. It swims a slow, helix'd path, there but demanding nothing. Obscured by floating leaves, then appearing again. They must have forgotten about this fish, left it behind and no one noticed. Maybe they just couldn't catch it, because it was so slippery, so strong. She should tell someone, she thinks.

She looks around; there is no one to tell. The fish is gone now, hidden again. Maybe they wouldn't even believe her. Or care. She'd tried to tell them about the fish before. How the fish was screaming, frightened, trapped. And how no one saw or helped. But her uncle was there, she told them, he heard her, saw her, so gentle to the little fish, so careful to take away the sharp hook and not cause any more pain. She'd tried to tell about his warm hands, holding her close. But her father needed to get to the drugstore for her brother's inhaler. Her mother on the phone, pleading, her sister threatening to leave rehab. They couldn't listen about the little fish. So she'd told another story. About her uncle driving her home, after their fishing trip. Just the two of them. He'd been paying such extra attention to her lately. Taking her for special adventures, special treats. Telling her she was such a good girl, she deserved it. Telling her she was very special to him. Her parents heard that part. So she kept telling. She told them about stopping for ice cream on the way home. About her uncle pulling off the road in the dark. About the fun game he wanted them to play together. She told them about frightened, about trapped, about pain. About his fat hands, and what they did to her. Her parents listened hard to that story. Paid attention. Such turmoil then. Her parents yelling into the phone, the threat of violence, of legal dispute. She heard her uncle's voice over the phone, the last time, pleading with her parents. Such a fuss she caused. And all hers, this time. Because she was so special. For a while. Her uncle exiled in the end, a small sacrifice. Banished alone to that tiny room. Like cutting loose and throwing back a wounded, bloodied little fish. But then it simply swims away, disappears below the smoothing surface. In the end, it's like nothing ever happened at all.

At least she never had to see him again, really, after their final special day. She never had to hear his voice ask her *Why? Why would you do that to me? Why would you lie?*

The fish emerges again, eyeing her. Its tail fin bumps a drifting, laden leaf; ashes float down and the fish catches them in its mouth as it glides past. She wonders how long it will glide there, along a shallow river current. Perhaps it will live to be a hundred. Always lurking, just waiting to bubble up, to emerge thrashing again and again.

No, she tells herself, eventually it will stop. Unfed, and all alone in the cold like that. She takes a deep breath, exhales. It has to die. It has to.

MUSICAL CHAIRS

"They call her the Senator's Wife," he tells me.

"Oh. So, you still want to be a senator?" I ask.

"Well, yeah. Eventually."

"And that's what your friends call her? 'The Senator's Wife'?"

"Mm."

"She's supportive. Well groomed. Law-abiding."

"Yeah." He shifts his weight, peeling himself away from me.

"She's beautiful."

"I think so," he says.

No. He doesn't need to affirm this; it is an objective analysis. She looks down on us from a cheap frame propped on a bookshelf, a shelf that still holds his adolescent and teenage books, here in his parents' house. I knew him in high school but never came to this house. There would have been no reason to, then. Now he is back from law school, pre–his own apartment, and we are having sex beneath a photo of his by-any-standards-beautiful fiancée, left waiting with pearls and chignon back in Georgetown.

I hate that I have to ask. "So, what about me? Why are you here, with me? What am I?" I am the Senator's Concubine, I'm dying to say, but that is too cute.

"You . . . " he says, tenderly stroking my sweaty hair, "are ambitious. You are going to achieve. You are going to do fucking amazing things, all on your own."

This is cruel, his faith in me. And inappropriate. At sixteen he was gawky and spotty and too smart for his own good, hyper-political, a frenzied blur. Debating Club, Junior State, the ranting editorial section of the school paper. All the soft and non-threatening civics of high school were mowed flat by his senatorial drive. I smiled indulgently, everyone did, then, at Chas's panting, socialist need to Do Something, at his angelic blond curls and beige corduroy slacks. I would have shunned a crush with cruel and condescending sweetness. I would have dismissed him, thoroughly. I have now made the mistake of layering that memory onto this present man, reencountered five weeks ago in a bar I thought him too unhip for, and have wound up here, naked in bed with someone who is no longer who he was. Who now calls himself Chuck. Who has, in sneaking a new self past me, into me, lied.

"Can I kiss you?" he asks in a skilled whisper, like it is a meaningful thing. This man could, will, become a senator. He is well beyond me and in total control, cool and self-assured as a fascist.

"Yes," I whisper back, grateful and hating myself, hating him.

It is October. His wedding is scheduled for June. In January, a sweater for him half-knit (yes, I knit, you asshole, I think), my hatred frayed as used yarn, I pick up some other guy I truly don't know in the hip bar, have sex in his car, and later call Chas to tell him he's fucked, that I never want to see him again, and to please return my copy of *One Hundred Years of Solitude* sometime when I'm not home. Because of this, I don't hear, a month later, of his engagement to the Senator's Wife abruptly ending when Chas decides he's just not ready to get married. She had moved here from Georgetown, bought the Vera Wang dress, registered at Williams-Sonoma. The cream-and-roses invitations had already gone out. I also don't hear of it because Chas doesn't call me again for three years.

SOMEHOW, THEN, WE become friends. Once every eighteen months or so we wind up in bed, resulting in six months of revived snarl and separation, but we always work our way back to close-knit. He always has an excuse, and it is always Timing. He might have fallen in love with me, yes, but the timing was always wrong: He was engaged, I was seeing someone else, he was seeing someone else, I was being a lesbian, he was living in San Francisco, one of us moved and couldn't find the other's new address or phone number. To him it would seem merely a matter of temporal misalignment. That we simply never fell into the solitude gaps in each other's lives. I think this is bullshit, but I let it stand; the truth doesn't flatter me. Years go by, and we go to the Frolic Room for drinks, to El Coyote for nachos, to the Nuart for Scorsese retrospectives. We applaud each other's successes and lacerate each other's antagonists. We riffle through other lovers. At some drunken point one evening he concedes that if we ever were together, really tried being together, yes, we'd wind up wanting to kill each other, but no, we wouldn't ever be bored. This is a tiny victory, shallow and insignificant though it may be. I burrow into it like a hastily dug grave.

I finish the sweater I once started for him and wear it myself. I wear it for years in front of him, carry it around, leave it lying in the hatchback of my car or draped over a chair until, finally, one chilly night we are sitting outside on the new balcony of my new condominium, and he is cold, and I can offer it to him. A retroactive, conceptual offering. Hey, this is great, he says, fondling it, Did you make this? For you, I tell him. A long, long time ago. He looks surprised, then abruptly seems to remember a meaningful thing. He nods, puts the sweater on, admiring my skill. Zosia, my new little dog, nudges him. I named her after my grandmother; I'd finally decided I was saving the name for no reason. Chas picks her up and nuzzles her in his lap. His fingers massage little circles in her fur; she closes her eyes blissfully and I am uncomfortably reminded of his fingers once touching me like that, those same little massaging circles.

MY NEW CONDO is beautiful, a result of my doing fucking amazing things, all on my own. High ceilings and hardwood floors. Stunning appointments, a desirable neighborhood south of the Boulevard in Sherman Oaks. I am the youngest person in the building, and the residents, many of them immigrants of forty and fifty years, still speaking with German and Polish and Yiddish accents, who came here with nothing and are now *comfortable*, treat me like a successful granddaughter and tell me they are happy the building has fresh blood. The next youngest are the two women who live next door, LouAnn and Bev, in their early forties, with Brooklyn accents and a lot of condo-oriented spirit; the three of us are elected president, vice-president, and secretary of the Homeowner's Association Board, which entitles us to receive late-night, distraught, heavily accented calls about plumbing problems and being locked out. LouAnn and I post friendly if slightly directive notices on the lobby bulletin board, announcing *Please Note: The Lobby Floor Will Be Waxed This Wednesday A.M., Watch Your Step!*, or *Please Note: Residents*

Must Park In Their Assigned Spaces—Visitor Parking Is For Visitors Only! A gentlemen couple in their fifties sneak treats to Zosia and insist I let them take her for walks; they tell me she is very ethereal for a poodle. One time I hear an old lady shrieking "Fire!" across the hallway, and I race to her aid with a fire extinguisher; her tea kettle, forgotten, had boiled out its water and the kettle's burning bottom was filling the kitchen with acrid black smoke. This sweet old lady, Mrs. Steinman, has a leg brace and a crumpled left arm, neither of which prevents her from taking out her own trash and doing all her own grocery shopping. In thanks for my blasting her kitchen with fire extinguisher foam, she leaves at my door three six-packs of Diet 7-Up, which she has wheeled upstairs to our floor in her little wire cart. She is from a tiny village in Poland, the same, we discover over 7-Up, as my grandmother Zosia. But my grandmother, daughter of the village rabbi, had fled the Russian pogroms; Mrs. Goldberg escaped as a limping, polio-afflicted twelve-year-old from the Germans. The village no longer exists. Her family no longer exists. I feel for her, having to live all on her own. I make it a point to engage with her in long chats when we meet.

One morning LouAnn calls me early, distraught, to tell me a swastika has been carved into our most recent posted notice.

"A swastika?" I repeat. I have never seen an actual one, in my own actual life. "Who here's going to creep downstairs in the middle of the night and put up a swastika?"

"I don't know. Bev's totally freaked. You know about her grandparents, right?"

"Yeah. . . . I can't believe this."

"And Mrs. Steinman saw it. She was hysterical. She started babbling in Polish."

"Oh, no."

"I'm going to call the cops. I'll call you back afterward." She hangs up.

CHAS IS IN therapy. He is turning over a new leaf. He told me about this several months ago, sitting on the balcony of my new condo, wearing the sweater I once knit for him. He's ready to settle down, make a commitment. He has just been made the chief trial attorney for the public defenders' office and spends a lot of time in court, yelling at judges, Doing Something. He is interviewed on radio and television, his liberal dervish energy much in demand, and is earning one-fourth of what he used to make as a corporate litigator. He tells me about the new girl he is seeing and uses the unfortunate metaphor of Musical Chairs to describe how he is now at a certain age, there is a certain point, there comes a time, something about the empty chair presented to you at the exact moment you feel compelled to sit down, how you take that chair. Like when the time comes, in life, I think, to just go ahead and buy yourself a condo. It is all about Timing.

She is bright and pretty and her SAT scores were higher than his, he tells me, although he doesn't give me the actual number. She is trying to make it as an actress and is really very, very talented. They have just found an apartment together—crappy, but with his pay cut and, you know, her money situation, it's not too bad.

We are at the edge of the evening where we usually either turn to sex or we do not, and at this exact moment he gets up to call her, to tell her he will be home soon. It's after two in the morning. Zosia looks at him, at me, hopefully, ignoring the impending implication of his empty chair. I pick her up. I'd always wanted a dog—this is the first home where I could have one. She has come into my life at just the right time.

"CHUCK SAYS YOU guys talked to the police?" Missy asks me in the kitchen; she has followed, helpfully, to help me pour the white wine.

"Yeah. After the fourth time they finally came and took a report."

"Wow . . . and this is such a nice neighborhood."

"This place is fucking great!" Chas yells from the living room. Missy and I join him, Zosia trotting after us. "I told you this place was great," he says to Missy as she hands him his wine. "Thank you, sweetie."

"It really is. It's beautiful," she says to me.

"Thanks." We sit on my new couch, my new chair. Missy leans over to run her veinless, tendonless hand along the gleaming hardwood floor. Their ratty new apartment, I know, is in a lesser area of Santa Monica and has shag chartreuse carpeting.

"Chuck says you looked at, what, like over a *hundred* condos?"

"Oh, thanks," I say to him. "Sure, make me look like that."

He shrugs. "You're selective. You're persistent. It paid off, you got the right place."

"Except for Nazi vandals."

"Dyslexic Nazi vandals," he says.

"Oh, yes," Missy says, "Chuck told me the swastikas are wrong?"

"They're backwards. I want to post a notice that says 'Learn to draw a proper swastika, you fascist prick'."

"You *stupid* fascist prick'," he adds.

"Oh, come on. I can just hear you, pleading this guy's case. 'Your Honor, this isn't a Nazi swastika! This is the ancient Aztec symbol of peace!'" I tell him, and he laughs.

"Is that really what it means?" Missy asks him. He nods. Zosia pushes a ball toward her; Missy pats her gingerly, then looks like she wants to wash her lovely, lotus-like hands.

"We're installing a surveillance camera," I tell them. "In the lobby."

"Is that legal?" Missy asks Chas. He nods again. "Okay, doggy, go on," she says.

"The cops suggested it to us."

"Sure, *they* don't have to pay for it," he says.

"It's going to cost the Association a few thousand dollars."

"Go on, doggy."

"Hey, come here, puppy. . . . " Chas picks up Zosia, to distract her from Missy.

"It's worth it. The whole building's terrified. We're the Jewish Home for the Aged here."

"It *is* terrifying," Missy says.

"It's a felony," he tells her.

"Really?"

"Four felonies," I point out. "Each one's a separate charge. Hate Crime Unit took the report. Of course, the detective made a point of telling me he didn't believe in 'hate crime' legislation. 'Why should burning a black church be any worse than burning anyone's home?'"

"Cops. . . . " Chas shakes his head.

"Excuse me, darling, you'd be the *first* to claim we violated the Nazis' civil rights by making the building too difficult to break in to," I tell him.

"You're actually denying him freedom of speech. Freedom of expression."

"You'd get this guy off?"

"Nah. I want to fry the bastard." He rubs Zosia behind the ears. "Woodja woodja woodja."

"You're the voice of the downtrodden. The defender of the oppressed, the victimized, the unwashed masses."

"Oh, you guys," says Missy, smiling.

"Yeah, but *you're* a dear friend," he says. "You catch him on video, I say screw the trial. Crucify him. Howsat? Howsat feel?" Zosia loves him madly. "I'd love to get a dog. Missy is not a dog person."

"Well . . ." she hedges, glancing at me. She is even more beautiful, I think, than Chas's earlier, dumped fiancée, the Senator's Wife in the looking-down-on-me photo. "This one's really cute, though," she says. "I could have one like this."

"There isn't another one like this," he tells her.

"That's very true. She's ethereal," I say.

"Terribly ethereal," he agrees.

"I'm knitting her a sweater," I announce.

"You are? That's so adorable!" Missy smiles at him, smiles at me. She is happy at becoming dear friends with Chas's dear friend and her dear little dog.

Chas follows me into the kitchen for more chips, the entire basket of which he and I have devoured but Missy hasn't touched. He hops up to sit on the counter while I tear open a fresh bag.

"You know, the comps on this place have already gone up," I tell him. "It's already worth maybe thirty thousand more than I paid."

"The perfect time to buy," he says. "You are very wise. You made a fucking brilliant choice."

As I pass with the basket he catches me within the V of his legs; I stop, and his knees tighten slightly at either side of my waist. I look down at the chips and he tugs me forward, rests his chin on top of my head. We stay this way for a moment, but I don't know what this is. Other than exactly a moment I wanted, and another thing to hate him for.

"Hey, you guys?" we hear Missy call. He takes his time releasing me, then lets me go ahead of him into the living room.

"OKAY, SO, THE next thing, you gotta set the timer right," Cliff tells us. Cliff is our surveillance specialist. He has installed a fake fire detector—we had been given a choice of fake fire detector, fake briefcase, or fake teddy bear—in the lobby, its tiny hidden camera cued on the bulletin board and wired to a monitor hidden in the storage room. "It tells you the date and time, shows it right on the video. Important for when you go to court." LouAnn and I nod, take notes. "How many times this goon show up?"

"Fourteen," LouAnn tells him. "We have fourteen flyers slashed with swastikas." LouAnn is keeping a file of them, all the dates listed, just as the police instructed. Every time one is swastika'd we immediately replace it, so all the residents coming on or off the elevator, collecting their mail, don't have to walk by it and get traumatized. Everyone is waiting, hoping, praying, they tell us, for this to end, for us to do something.

"He does it sometime between midnight and 6:00 AM. Every third or fourth night," I say.

"We thought about staking out the lobby ourselves, but . . ."

"No, no, you ladies are doing the right thing." Cliff checks his watch and programs in the correct date and time. "You don't want anyone getting hurt. You get him on camera, that's it, you got him. He's not getting away with shit."

LouAnn and I return to the lobby to post a brand-new notice: *Please Note: Do Not Buzz Anyone Into The Building You Do Not Know Or Expect Personally! We Must Look Out For Each Other!* We stand for a moment, looking at the fake fire detector. She waves at it like a tourist.

"This is creepy," she says. "Every time we get on and off the elevator, we're being watched."

"I know. But I feel like I'm being watched, anyway. Every time I take Zosia for a walk at night, or just going into the garage. Who knows when this guy is hanging around or not? When he's going to show up next time?"

"How about what he's going to *do* next time? I keep waiting for it to get worse."

"Me, too," I say. "I'm not sleeping at night. I keep waking up, all the time. Every little noise . . . I feel like we're all so *vulnerable*."

"We *are*," she says. The elevator opens, and we get in. "I mean, c'mon, we have a building full of dykes, kikes, fags, and cripples. This guy could have a field day."

"I'm only half-kike," I remind her, and she laughs.

I WANT SO badly to hate her; the best I can do is to feel bored. Despite the SAT scores, which I continue to be told were very, very high; her intelligence is responsive, the bright and supportive follow-ups in conversation. It doesn't matter. She is sweet and sincere, with Edwardian curls, bird-like bones, and healthy pink gums. She is delicate, sweatless. She answers the phone when I call him at home and keeps me there for long minutes, asking a vast range of personal questions, revealing private details, creating intimacy between us. Eventually she stops turning the phone over to him at all and goes ahead to make the plans herself, for the three of us. Eventually I stop asking to speak to him at all and succumb to the girlfriend chat. She is insultingly unthreatened.

The three of us go to dinner at El Coyote, where Chas and I each finish two double margaritas before our Numero Ocho combo platters arrive. Missy delicately picks the canned green beans from her vegetarian tostada.

"So, you got him?" he asks, excited. "That's great, you got him. I love it."

"Yeah. Three different nights on tape. At 2:33, 2:41, and 2:27 AM."

"Nazis are very punctual."

"At one point he actually stops, turns his head, looks right at the camera. LouAnn and I were sure he figured it out. But then he turns and carves a *second* one."

"Balls. Big, Nazi balls."

"Chuck said none of you recognize him, right?" asks Missy.

"Nope. He's some fat, schlubby, thick-necked guy. He's wearing the same T-shirt and shorts every time. And he's totally blasé about it, just strolls in. . . . "

"That's so gross," Missy says.

"At least we're *doing* something about it. The video thing was brilliant."

"You're Simon Wiesenthal. You're Beate Klarsfeld," Chas pounds a fist on the table in tribute.

"And this schlubby guy . . . I'd always pictured some well-groomed, goose-stepping Aryan eating streusel and drinking Riesling."

"No, the Nazi from *Cabaret*," Chas says. "That beautiful, sweet, blond angelic kid, who gets up in the tavern and sings 'Tomorrow belongs, Tomorrow belongs'—"

"Tomorrow belongs to *meeee!*" I join in singing, and the two of us raise our margarita glasses like beer steins. "Did we rent that, or what?"

"No, Beverly Cinema."

"Oh, yeah, with the guy at the ticket window—"

"With the hair!"

"Yeah!"

"I saw that movie once," says Missy, smiling. "It was really good."

We all smile and sip our drinks.

"So. . . . " Chas says.

"So, anyway, tonight the cops are finally staking us out. They'll grab him in the act. LouAnn and I are going to wait up. I want to see this guy suffer."

"You know, even with the videos they'll plead him down. You'll probably wind up with a few counts of vandalism, deface-ment of property, maybe a terrorism statute. Misdemeanors. He could even get off."

"Then we'll form a posse, track him down, and string him up by his hairy Nazi balls."

"You'll let me know, right? You'll call me tomorrow?"

"You don't want me to call at 2:47 AM?"

"Nah. I'm in court early." He gets up, heads to the bathroom. "Order me another, right?"

Missy and I smile at each other.

"Chuck told me how much he loved your book," she says to me.

"Really?" I ask, although he and I have already discussed it. He calls me every few days from his office. It is when we talk. I decide not to tell her this. I decide to spare her.

"Yeah," she says. "He told me he thought it was incredible. I can't wait to read it."

"I hope you like it."

"Oh, I know I will. Wow. . . . " She sighs, takes a sip of her margarita. "I wish I could get it together. Maybe I should go to grad school. I don't know. I just think it's incredible, everything you're doing. Both of you." She gazes toward the bathroom; Chas is on his way back to us. She leans a little closer to me. "I feel so insignificant," she says quietly.

I want to throw my drink in her face. No, I want to claw her first, rake my nails across her creamy cheek, so the alcohol burns.

"Hey, sweetie," Chas says to her.

"No, wait, I'm going next." She slides out of the booth. "Chuck, finish my margarita." She heads to the bathroom, calling back to me: "I'm *such* a lightweight!"

"How's Zosia?" Chas asks.

"She's delicious."

"I'm converting to Judaism," he tells me.

"You are?"

"Yeah."

"You are."

"Monday I begin instruction with the Janowsky family rabbi."

I suddenly get it. "You're getting married."

He nods. "Next August somethingth."

"You're a devout atheist."

"It means something to her. Kids and everything. It's okay. I like Jews."

"What does your therapist say?"

"He approves. Well, he *did*. I'm not seeing him anymore." He pours half of Missy's margarita into my glass and the rest into his. He raises his glass. "*L'chaim*."

We drink, and the salt burns my lips. Missy returns.

"*Mazel tov*," I tell her.

"Oh. . . . " She slides in next to him, smiling, and slips her arm into his. "He told you. *I* wanted to tell you. . . . " She playfully punches his arm. "I'm so excited. I can't wait."

"I bet . . . well, indeed, a big, fat, hairy *mazel tov*."

"Thanks," they say together. He takes her lovely hand and she lifts her head to kiss him, perfectly on the lips, her white throat delicately arched. I think, unwelcomingly, of the last time I went down on him, my desperate, inelegant head-bobbing. Give me a chance, I want to say, one chance to do it over. I'll do it right this time, be everything you want, all of it, achieve everything, for you.

"OKAY, ARE YOU ready for this?" LouAnn asks. She is calling from her office; she is just off the phone with the police. "Claudio Marcelo Petrello, he's thirty-one, he's from Argentina, he's here illegally."

"You're kidding."

"No, wait. He's Italian, and they told me his parents, or maybe his grandparents, I don't remember, were fascists who fled Italy after the fall of Mussolini's regime."

"What? He told them that?"

"That's what the cops just said." Six hours earlier, at 2:57 AM, we had awakened when a police helicopter, two black-and-whites, two squad cars, two plainclothes detectives, and four uniformed cops stormed our building. I'd grabbed Zosia, put on her little sweater, and taken her into LouAnn and Bev's place to watch from their balcony overlooking the street. Other people in our building were on their balconies, too, in bathrobes and slippers, hiding their faces in curtains and shadows, still terrified. When they looked up and saw us, they'd waved, given us thumbs-ups. This morning Mrs. Steinman posted a "Thank-You" card on the bulletin board.

"You know how he got in the building? He had a fucking *key*. He's a delivery guy for *The Wall Street Journal*."

"A *paper* boy?"

"He's been here every night for five months, delivering the paper to Mr. Weiner on the second floor. And they asked him why he did it, right? He said he was mad the elevator wasn't working that one time. That we were too cheap to fix it."

"Sure, that makes sense."

"He's already out on bail. Fifty grand."

"I'd like to rip his throat open. Stone him to death. Something biblical."

"Me, too. Oh, and get this, the cops almost *missed* him. They were just going to wait until 3:00 AM and then leave. He showed up just in time."

CHAS ANSWERS THE phone.

"Hi, it's me," I say.

"Hey," he says exuberantly. "So, so? What happened?"

"Is Missy home?"

There is something in my voice; his voice drops, subdues. "No, she's out. I can talk."

"Tell me you're madly in love. Tell me you're blissfully happy. Tell me she's everything you've ever wanted." I stop, awaiting a sentence.

He breathes, carefully. "Yes, I'm madly in love. And I'm blissfully happy. And no, she isn't everything I've ever wanted."

"What isn't she?"

"She isn't . . ."

"What? What? What *isn't* she? Tell me."

"It's not what she isn't. That's okay. What she *is* works. It'll work."

"It'll 'work'."

"Yeah."

"I don't understand. I don't get how you can say you're madly in love, but she's not everything you want, and then wrap it up with 'It'll work'."

"I'm ready for it. What works for me is different now, I've changed a lot. It's the right time."

"You're sitting down, that's all."

"What?"

"The music's fucking stopped, and you're tired, and you just want to sit down."

"I have to go."

We both hang up.

CLAUDIO MARCELO PETRELLO, at his arraignment, hears the felony charges dropped to four counts of vandalism and four counts of defacement of property. They are all misdemeanors, with the slim possibility of a few months in county jail, or a few hundred dollars' fine, but, the city attorney whispers later to us, he will most likely receive a suspended sentence and probation. His bail is reduced to five thousand dollars, to the delight of his family members gathered in the courtroom, a schlubby, thick-necked mother and father and siblings. All of this is due to the fact that Claudio has no prior offenses, and there was no one-on-one threat of physical violence to anyone, and no permanent destruction to the building. It was all superficial, the damage. A trial date is set for next month. The Petrello family dances out of court; LouAnn and Bev, Mrs. Steinman, Mr. Weiner, some other residents and I are seated in the back of the room, trying to be invisible. We still feel afraid. But Claudio does not even glance at us; it is entirely possible, we realize, entirely probable, that he has no idea who we are.

"This is it?" says Mrs. Steinman. "This is the worst that happens to this man?" She is furious, tearful.

"Well," says LouAnn, "at least we can start sleeping at night."

"Maybe we can get *The Wall Street Journal* to reimburse us for the video equipment," I say.

"I want an explanation for this," says Mrs. Steinman. "I want this man to look me in the face and tell me why. Why he would do such a thing. I don't understand."

LouAnn shrugs. "Maybe we'll hear it at the trial. Maybe it'll make more sense."

A FEW MONTHS later, Missy calls.

"Hi, honey," she says. "God, we haven't talked to you in so long! How is everything?"

"Fine," I say. "How are you doing?"

"Oh, Chuck's working crazy hours, you know. Oh, and he's running for City Council, did we tell you that?"

"Ah. Great. Landslide. He's on his way. He'll rule the world."

"I know," she says proudly. "I'm trying to help him as much as I can. I'm working part-time at his office. *And,* doing all the wedding stuff, you know. There's so much to do, it's great, it's keeping me busy. The invitations go out next month. Is there anybody you want to bring?"

"Zosia?"

"Oh, I wish. No dogs allowed," she says with a laugh. "It's going to be beautiful. It's going to be amazing."

"Oh, I bet."

"That's actually why I'm calling. I'm trying to decide what to get Chuck for a wedding present, and I figure you know him so well. . . . I know you're really busy, but would you go looking with me? I have a couple of ideas. . . . "

"Sure," I say. "Why not?"

"I was thinking maybe this Saturday. If you have time. Oh, I wanted to ask you, whatever happened to the Nazi guy? The one they caught?"

"He's gone. He never showed up for trial."

"Really?"

"He took off for Argentina. Well, he's gone, so that's what the cops think. They'll never find him."

"Wow. Well, at least it's over. At least you can get on with your life."

"Right."

"So, anyway," she says, "come on, I need your brain. You should know. What would make him happy? What does Chuck really want?"

MULTIPLE CHOICE

He spotted her immediately from—his word—afar. The Famous

    a) Playwright
    b) Congressman
    c) Musician

had espied her sylvan, fragile beauty at once, he tells her on their first date, an old-Hollywood-glam steakhouse, sanguine leather booths and five à la carte asparagus spears for twelve dollars, and heels and nail polish and mascara she was unused to but felt circumstances demanded, these unique circumstances, having been singled out, discerned, plucked from the madding crowd by this Renowned and Brilliant Man. It was her singular grace, he says, that he could not help noticing—even from afar, yes—the delicate strain of tendons at her throat, the soul-rich, beckoning light from her eyes as she

   a) listened to the staged reading of his new, long-awaited play, a drama of history's oppressed women now empowered, resurrected from obscurity, the unrelenting theme of his canon (and she has long admired the unabashed passion of his work, never mind the ticket/donation at the fund-raiser for a local women's shelter was the equivalent of seventeen days' rent),

   b) licked envelopes at his grassroots reelection campaign HQ (the drudge role she'd volunteered for to flesh out alone-but-not-lonely weekends, although a sincere admirer of his legislative agenda, of course, his long-ago, one-term House of Representatives crusade for the rights of the poor and meek of his district and the earth),

   c) sat by herself front row at his comeback coffeehouse concert, twirling a thin lock of hair (and tears welling to those heart-beating, heart-breaking lyrics of his, admiring the chivalric warble in his voice, his

troubadour's promise of courtly love and eternal-
though-tortured devotion in all those unironic,
yearning songs of her yearning adolescence),

and so he had to seize the rare and precious moment, he tells her.
He had no choice. He could not allow this recognized *her* to just
slip by and away. So that is why he sent, could not help sending

a) his personal assistant
b) an intern
c) a roadie

to approach her, proffer the invitation to this dinner, something
he is still apologizing for over a purple gash of tenderloin. I didn't
mean to be disrespectful, he swears. I didn't mean to have you
summoned. You are not some random

a) fan
b) constituent
c) groupie

to me, not at all. I was intimidated by you, he confides. I am just so
out of practice at being back in the world these days. Forgive me?

But there is no need for apology; she understands, is sure
of his assessment. It confirms her most secret, or hoped-for,

sense of her true value, her rarified self. She knows she is not some incidental happy-hour appetizer, the careless newsstand grab of a free weekly. She suspects she is superiorly intelligent, despite a lack of obvious results, a showy CV or lucrative job that would finally unburden her of those student loans. Her beauty is subtle but evident to the discerning eye, an eye her thirteen past lovers/boyfriends/FWBs had never quite honed. Her potential is simmering—there will be a top-tier graduate school down the road, she assures herself, or a wildly creative flowering, perhaps a dedicated career with an environmental nonprofit—gaining its strength and unique bouquet, and look, here at last is a man who has recognized her incipient exceptionality, an older, wiser, ways-of-the-world man, with a *parfumier's* sophisticated nose and an appreciation of quiet style. She forgives him his clumsy gaffe. But, emboldened, she encourages his unease. She puts him graciously in his place; of *course* she does not trust him, she tells him, given his reputation. Of course she is suspicious, given his timing, this sudden return-splash to the public eye of his. Are you now truly

a) sober?

b) legally divorced?

c) drug-free?

she queries. Is his act really together now, is he sincere? She eval-
uates his responses with stern professorial squints. She offers
insightful critique of his faults. He is eager, flustered, little-
boyish, cannot finish his steak, urges her to doggy-bag it and
the remaining asparagus spear home. He would think less of her
were she *not* so wary of him, he tells her, and he is grateful for
both her spirit and her open mind. He is delighted by her integ-
rity. She does not even know how powerful she is. He will prove
himself, if she will just give him a chance. They agree he is worthy, or at least potentially so, and she agrees to bestow upon him
more of her precious, rarified time.

ON THEIR SECOND date—rare, unsustainable sushi—he
reveals his deepest-pain story, what once triggered and drove his
legendary self-destructiveness but has also and since been the
fueling, bolstering heartthrob of his life's work. She has heard
the story before—she once viewed long, channel-surfing seconds of a cable documentary on him, his struggle to overcome
the distressful childhood to Make Something of Himself—
but that is just superficial, salivating press, he tells her, media
mumbo jumbo, the Journalism 101 exercise unable to penetrate
mere persona. No, he must share his most intimate self with her,
alone; he cannot hide from her his private pain, not if he wishes
her to understand, or—far more important—to reveal her *own*

pain, the pain he sees in her soul-bruised eyes, the pain he does so fervently wish her to share, to trust him with, and so he cannot help telling her himself about

a) his sister, older, adored, and the ripening scent of womanhood he went boyhood sniffing for, her female bathroom smell, black soapy hairs in the tub drain and sticky panties in the hamper, how she stumbled past his bedroom door late that one night, a yell to the sleepy, unwatchful parents that she was home safe from her date, how he lay silent and listening and heard her enter her room, heard the door close and the click of the lock, heard her window creak open slowly, deliberately slow, heard her stumble-crawl through and out to disappear again and the slow, disappearing roll of tires on pavement and then she was disappeared forever, stolen taken abducted, an abandoned car found with a mere smear of her blood but they never found her, more of her or her body, and he is tormented to this day forever by her absence and absent scent, for his silence that fateful night, for not watching over her, keeping her at home, safe,

b) his mother, so unmoored after his *good-riddance godless dog of a* father was gone for good this time, and he was five years old, six, the *Man of the House*, she'd whisper, *Sleep with me tonight, honey, you'll protect me, won't you?* and he grew yearning and used to her moist nylon nightie heat and oniony whiff, seven years old, eight, but how he came home that one day to the sound of urgent naked flesh-struggle inside, how he burst in and hurled himself brave at her naked hairy attacker, but then she screamed at him—at him! —to *Stop it, goddamn it, stop, get out*, grabbing and holding *him* down, pulling down his pants and her angry hand smacks, slamming on his naked buttocks, her damp, naked white breasts shuttling across his back and being banished to his little-boy room to listen listen listen to her with that pumping swarthy man, then to her with all the other come-and-go scumbag men, those animals, while he'd sweat and grope and pump at himself and could not protect her from her own degradation, the descent into slattern filth and booze and drugs and final vein-burned fate and he was truly left all alone for good,

c) the woman he found, he was innocent childhood backwoods exploring that day, was all, branches for a fort or Y-stick to fashion a slingshot, when he stumbled, tripped, was tripped up by the thick twig of a blue-veined marble arm beneath brown leaves, the nest of dark clotted hair, what he had to describe and relive over and over, how he fell onto and thus found the chilling torn body, his scream-ing screaming for someone to come, till his hoarse cries were heard and he was found, curled on top of her naked sweet rot, fingers gripping her hair, her cold face, her icy breasts. An unknown, unidenti-fied woman, they told him afterward, some random no-name Jane Doe, some fated whore, just a body a body a body used and broken and discarded by bad, brutal men.

And she takes his trembling hand, I am here, she tells him ten-derly, *I am here*, and he clutches, grips, weeps over his fatty toro.

I was right about you, he says. But how can I earn you? You could have any man in the world. How can I deserve so much grace?

EXPANSIVE, CRYSTAL-VASED FLOWER arrangements are delivered, overwhelm her studio apartment with their cloying lily gasp. Parchment and ink missives arrive each day, for he eschews the digital chilliness of social media or text. He buys her a several-months'-rent dress she reluctantly accepts but cannot imagine wearing anywhere but some grand event he might escort her to, someday. He offers to get her transmission fixed, to pay her rent, pay off her debts, then delightedly begs her forgiveness when she refuses with huffy pride, is giddy when she sends back the pearl-and-platinum choker in its iconic robin's-egg-blue box. He takes her to

a) the taping of a program for NPR, the interviewer rhapsodizing on his cultural legacy, his role as a shaper of American theater and recontextualized, contemporized historical perspective, the much-needed reemergence of his moral vision, his voice,

b) a parking-lot rally in support of migrant workers and undocumented immigrants, where the verbal sway of his impassioned rejoinders to xenophobic right-wing picketers and his impromptu Bible-quoting debate on the defining Christian tenet of shared brotherhood gets spontaneous applause, gets primetime network and then viral airplay,

c) an added date for his comeback concert, now becoming an actual tour, now a sold-out amphitheater full of nostalgic boomers and cynical hipsters seeking honed arrows for their toughened hearts, celebrating the rediscovery of his wandering-minstrel lyricism and authenticity,

while she stands to one privileged insider side and smiles and nods her support in response to his anxious, searching-for-her-in-the-pauses eyes. Afterward he is exhilarated but dismissive of the hoopla and noisy acclaim—It is not about that, he tells her, the joy is knowing she was there, with and for him. It was, paradoxically, a moment of their greatest intimacy thus far. He strokes her arm, intimately, describes to her the

a) upstate New York estate he will purchase for her, after this play goes Broadway and Tony and Pulitzer, with verdant grazing land for goats and long, hand-in-hand private walks and she can fill her days making chèvre or going to grad school and getting a doctorate in whatever discipline she likes, while he writes and writes, for the greatest, most inspired work of his life still lies ahead, he knows that now, and evenings before a roaring stone fireplace with wolfhounds or babies at their feet he will read those fresh-inspired pages aloud to her, his Lover, his Muse,

b) Georgetown townhouse they will make their havened own, when this campaign is done and won and he rises to and wins the next-on-the-list prize, a Senate seat, and he will storm the capital on behalf of the downtrodden and disenfranchised while she volunteers at animal shelters and veterans' hospitals and church soup kitchens, raises their golden children and elegantly DC-hostesses at his side, his Dolly, his Eleanor, his gracious helpmeet bride,

c) charming Craftsman bungalow they will settle in after this album drops and he's back on steady rotation, a giant Stickley bed and early-L.A. architecture like the profiles in those heavy, high-gloss magazines, and daytimes he will compose and record epic love songs dedicated to her in his state-of-the-art studio out back while she writes poems or novels or paints or sculpts or weaves or has kids, she can do anything she wants, for she is an Artist, too, his Brilliant Other,

the woman he cannot wait to introduce to the world as his. And every night they will make love for hours in mutual ecstasy and he will hold her safe in his arms while they weep gratitude for the relief of their shared pain, their island-in-the-stream togetherness, for their—his word—metamorphosizing love.

She coughs. Let's maybe take this a little slow, she tells him, a little nervous. Okay? And let's just keep this between us for now? You are a public figure, but I am a very private sort of person, I guess. I guess I'm not used to all this.

Of course, he assures. He knows what he offers is overwhelming, intense. He respects her privacy, her delicate sensibility. Everything will be up to her; everything will be hers. He is happy to give her as much time as she needs, although it is wrenching, excruciating for him to rein in his racing, galloping heart. He senses she finds him slightly ridiculous, and perhaps he even is. But he is serious, he insists. And he is somewhat hurt, to be honest—a brief shadow to his face—by her lingering skepticism. But she will see. She will open herself to him. She will learn to trust again. And then, once they are truly, fully faithed together, he will achieve his Greatest Things. She will at last be fully, deservedly realized in the world. And he leaves her at her apartment door, merely hand-kissed and cheek-stroked.

I am delighted to court you, he says.

And she is a little grateful for the reprieve, his willingness to keep resetting the clock at courtship and tentative, respectful ladyfair kisses goodnight, and she is—increasingly very—relieved because she tries but cannot ignore the age difference, the lack of actual attraction or sexual pull, or even the faint but growing, creeping-in crawl and distaste at the smell of his skin and breath and hair—when, she wonders, does *older* merely become old?—and she is happy to encourage this urgently leisurely pace to give her time to adjust, adapt, yes, that's all she needs, because this vision and dangle of an existence lived at such peaks, such unbound emotional extravagance, is of course overwhelming, just as he says. A touch of altitude sickness is all.

But what if he is right, she wonders, worries, and this is the—one? only?—call to liberation from negligibility, her gifted destiny revealed at last, her inevitable grand role to play, the ultimate Wikipedian narrative arc of her life?

HER FRIENDS AND co-workers and parents voice hesitant—envy-tinged, she suspects, or is that surprise at his choosing, at this sudden starshine upon her plain Jane face?—concerns; what about his past, they ask her, those old, vague pre-TMZ rumors of addictions and instability and bitter divorces and breakdowns and adolescent run-ins with the law?

Exactly, that is *past*, she assures them. It is Ancient History 101, it is why he disappeared from the public stage for so long, to confront his demons and finally work all that through. He has been totally upfront and honest about everything, and hasn't he channeled his furious, damaged genius into positive action and change? Look at what he is creating in the world—hasn't he risen above such skeptical misunderstanding, such hurtful snark? It is the price of greatness, she supposes to them, sighing, the burden of his brilliance. She allows her own voice to be tinged with status, with ascendency, and the next night shows up determinedly and steeled by Two Buck Chuck Chardonnay at his door to offer herself in reward.

IT IS HER fault, she feels, the awkward and unsync'd grapple of it, then the ultimate, mortifying failure. He is unable because of her lingering bourgeois superficiality, she is sure, her tentative, going-through-the-sexual-motions motions. Chemistry is, well, just *chemicals*, she chides herself, just Bunsen burner hype, schoolgirl mythology. Get over it. Love is of spirit and souls, and so if her flesh is passive, unmoved—cringes, actually—and her lungs strain for air during his groping, mewling, her-pleasure-is-everything exertions, it is no wonder the potency of his own response is weakened, disempowered, if his own pleasure in her is dulled. She apologizes.

He does not accuse her—on the contrary, he revels in her refinement, contrasts her constantly with other women, the coarse, withholding, pedestrian past

a) girlfriends

b) wives

c) lovers

in whom he placed such mistaken, disappointed faith, who could not rise to meet him at his level of essential truth. He understands she is not yet fully his—a subtle darkening of his voice—but he assures her she is making progress, justifying his trust. He has peeled for her his very soul to pulp and seeds and she cups it so soft in her dear hands. Whatever else he may achieve in this life, his only true dream is to die in her arms. She alone is his last chance for a profound happiness. She has not run, has not fled, and he needs no greater reassurance or evidence of the redemptive promise of her love.

She clears her throat. She wills herself to pat, no, stroke his shoulder, his naked back, to initiate, but he stops her,

No, he says. There will be plenty of time. They will get there soon, together. He has no doubt. It is their fate.

ONE LATER NIGHT—ANOTHER wilting, truncated effort—he asks her, yet again, to share her pain. Her most visceral, damaging pain, the pain she hides from the world but he can discern and will rescue her from, what will at last fuse their souls and thus, successfully, their flesh. He needs this from her. But she can think of no pain worthy enough to share. She tries to remember the agonies of spirit she must have suffered when that

a) sweet, senior-year-of-college boyfriend backed out on the eve of moving in, he just wasn't ready, he said, although she was really awesome and everything and he cared about her, and maybe he was just panicking, yeah, although didn't that show his unreadiness to make a commitment, even to a really great girl like her, and while it did hurt at the time, of course, her truest distress was having cleaned out her closet to make room for him and his stuff and it was too late to get those clothes back from Goodwill,

b) cubicle co-worker she hooked up with and started dating after the office Groundhog Day pub gathering confessed he was also sleeping with Anita in Human Resources, but she kept dating him for another few months anyway, because while it did hurt at the time, of course, what she secretly hoped was Anita would feel guilty enough to push forward a raise or promotion for her, and it went on until the day he just disappeared from their cubicle to go back and live with his parents in one of the Dakotas, Anita told her, rolling her eyes, over their let's-split-a-chicken-Caesar lunch,

c) hot wannabe actor guy from the CinemaSoape Laundromat—who she was sort of crazy about, or maybe was just crazy about the carnal sex and his pliable porno assurance with her body, although she nursed a hope this was or could be or would be love, but what would she do with this life-as-it-comes kid she could never introduce to her friends, her parents, even after he groomed the scruff and she bought him a decent jacket and pair of shoes— agreed to her ending it with nothing more than a carefree grin and insulting shrug, and while it hurt at the time, of course, when he offered to fuck her one final time in her car, she simply shrugged back and said Sure.

She is embarrassed by her lack of formative anguish. She feels shame at the juvenile unworthiness of her prior men, the mere and interchangeable boys she had chosen, those petty hurts; he will reassess her, realize she lacks profundity, a poet's tender heart. When he continues to entreat she demurs, mysteriously, hintingly, as if still clutching to her delicate breast the most ineffable of torments, as if he has not quite yet earned the peeling open of her soul, and at his now darkened, newly hardened face, at the twitch in his eye, she wonders, suddenly a little afraid, how much time she has left.

ONE MANY-NIGHTS-LATER NIGHT he calls. He is rambling, a thick-throated, inchoate stumble over sentences and words and it crosses her mind—as fear? as hope?—that he must be drunk, wasted, in the middle of some kind of breakdown,

Are you all right? she breaks in. Slow down, what are you saying, I cannot understand you.

He gulps, edges consonants, asks if she has ever

a) been assaulted, taken against her will, she can tell him, such violation can happen to any woman, one never blames the victim, she is never asking for it, never seeking to be overpowered or hurt that way, even if there was no actual physical force he would understand because there is always always the threat and so the woman must submit, in the end, must spread herself wide and perhaps even take pleasure in it, sometimes that happens, it is no fault of the woman if she gets aroused, wet, orgasms climaxes comes, a woman's body is designed that way, after all, to shudder and writhe and be possessed by the male force, and so she must confess, tell him all about it,

b) had sex with a black guy, a Mexican or a Muslim, or a dog, what is the ugliest, most filthy, diseased thing she has ever allowed inside her, been penetrated by, taken in to her most sacred private places, sucked or fingered or fucked, because some women, very sick and disturbed women, do crave and seek out such self-punishing, unnatural defilement and so she must confess, tell him all about it,

c) been paid for sex, whored herself out for cash or drugs or tuition, but doesn't every woman do that, in some way, sell herself for gutter slut cheap, because even the smart-negotiated exchange for marriage or caviar or jewels is still just perfumed, marked-up whoring, a piece of rotten meat with fancy sauce and price tag slapped on, just coldhearted, frigid, viper-bitch betrayal, and so she must confess, tell him all about it,

and he will try but cannot promise to forgive, although he may never be able to touch her again he can at least help her to repent, to cleanse herself, and so—Do not *ever*—there is vomit thickening her own throat now—*ever* contact me again, she says, and hangs up.

SHE NURSES HER nausea with quarts of ginger tea. She asks her landlord to turn up the water heater and scalding-showers herself every day, loofahs her crawling skin to a tender-bright new. There is a mailbox slew of fattened fine-stationery envelopes addressed in a blotty, barely legible scrawl she tears up without opening. There are sobbing voicemails and then heated, imploring texts, and she changes her phone number. There are emails with exclamation-point subject lines, and she marks them as spam, then deletes without reading. There are FedEx'd boxes she refuses to accept, although the nonplussed FedEx guy tells her there is no point, he cannot register her refusal or return to sender. There are deliveries of towering, long-stemmed vases and old-fashioned boxed bouquets she drops off at the nearest Cancer Treatment Center. She leaves the still gift-tagged, grand-event dress with a fancy consignment shop—a touch of guilt at not donating to some charity auction, but even her thirty percent share of the sale will help her cover last month's bills, this month's rent. She casually mentions to her friends and co-workers and parents that it is simply over, ended, is all—the age difference, sure—aiming for a shrugging, just-a-fling, nothing-to-see-here tone, but they continue to reference, to ask if she

a) has heard the rave notices and hot buzz for the L.A. previews of his play, about the record advance ticket sales for its Broadway run, the announcement of film rights already purchased by a legendary director for an Oscar-winning actress and that he has signed an above-the-title-credit, multi-million-dollar deal to write the screenplay,

b) has seen the polls predicting a landslide victory, the pundits proclaiming this is just the beginning, or new beginning, the resurrection of his political career and a nation's hope, a validation of progressive faith-based humanism, there is already talk of his keynote spot at the Convention, his Party-favorite, front-runner status for the next Senate seat, and who knows what political heights after that,

c) knows the first single off the new album has already made download history and a *Rolling Stone* cover piece is due next month, that a retrospective boxed set of his albums is in the works with all proceeds going to school arts programs, that he is organizing and headlining an upcoming HBO concert to benefit impoverished families and the children of famine,

and she ratchets up her shruggy indifference until they cease. She goes off-line, limits herself to local TV news of weather and sig alerts and petty neighborhood break-ins and eventually sleeps through the night, finally comes and goes from her apartment without first peepholing or peering up and down the street with queasy, galloping heart.

SIX MONTHS LATER an innocently thin, return-address-less, bulk-stock envelope slips from a sheaf of junk mail and she opens it without thinking. *I ask nothing of you,* it says, the penmanship lucid and precise, *I cannot even ask your forgiveness. But you must know I was very ill. The stresses of my second-chance fortune broke me; the challenge of you triggered a renewed haunting by my past. I abused you in an unforgivable manner and it is the loss of you that has at last shattered my denial and forced me to confront my darkest self, to seek help from*

a) *my AA sponsor. I am going to meetings every day, living one day at a time, it is so hard but so true, I finally understand the rigorous commitment it takes to lead an honest and real life, and I have no choice,*

b) *a spiritual advisor. I have found a priest, a brilliant Jesuit who understands me and my struggle, is guiding my return to faith, helping me choose and commit to an honest path forward, one grounded in harmony and peace, for*

c) *a shrink, a real psychiatrist. I cannot take meds with my history, but I am fully committed to the therapeutic process, grueling as it is, because I have finally chosen to be honest with myself about myself, and*

it is time to change my life. Your discretion and respect for my privacy these past months are proof of your extraordinary compassion, and I would be honored (although I have no right to be honored) if you would attend the (ticket enclosed) upcoming

a) *opening night*
b) *election night*
c) *concert*

and celebration event as my respected guest and my tender, tender friend.

HE STANDS SPOTLIGHTED and dignified and steady-spined before the applauding world, and she can see, even from a distance, the fresh serenity to his face, the clear and buoyant light in his eyes. But she can also discern—she alone, she is sure—the fragility behind his soft-murmured *Thank yous*, the frightened boy-child pulse. She applauds with the crowd, palms slapping hard and then harder, hoping he will

sense her forgiving and respectful presence, her support, perhaps notice she is wearing the (retrieved) dress he once gifted
her, and when their eyes catch—*You are here!* she alone can
hear him say—his dignified smile is suddenly a child's joyous
beam, humble and without guile.

He holds out his hand. Heads and cameras turn, rippling
the crowd with expectation. He is reaching, hoping, and she
finds herself—she cannot leave him just standing there, no—
stepping forward, then at his side. He seizes her hand, pulls
her closer, and announces to the applauding world: This is the
angel who has graced and saved me and made everything possible, the answer to my prayers. Here she is, the woman who
has changed my life.

HE UNDRESSES HER that night as if unwrapping an heirloom
ornament from sepia tissue leaves, and as she lowers herself
below him to the bed, as she opens to him her mouth, her arms,
her thighs, as she feels him slide hard inside her with startling,
spearing depth, she hears his soft voice murmur, whisper, tell
her, what she will do now is

a) pretend, pretend he is a stranger, a man of steel com-
mand, she has been carried off and she will struggle
while he positions and binds her, she will cry out

and beg while she is torn and split wide—show me, he says, show me how you bleed—and only then can he, will he, hear her screams and relent, will he soothe and stroke and take her so very tenderly,

b) force him to all fours, make him crawl and howl like a dog, like the ugly animal he is, she will tame him, shame him, beat him down to dirt, will fuck him with—see, he has the tool she must use, it straps on—all her own animal rage and pain, and only when he is fully degraded can he, will he, take her, find pleasure in her, for only then will she be brought down as foul and brutal and bestial as he,

c) lie still, stripped naked and serene, she will lie in the cold water bath—see, there is the snowy crushed ice he will pack her in so velvet soft—and when she is chilled fully and pure to white-blue porcelain flesh, she mustn't move, no shivering, no chattering, she must not spoil his pleasure, only then can he, will he, pound his heat into her, bring her back to a hot throbbing life,

and only then will they be truly together at last, only then will she fulfill her destiny, her fate.

She struggles against his weight, pulls her body from his clutch, is elated at her flesh resealing shut against him, at the strength of her simmering, resurging self. She breaks his final hold on her wrist, grabs and pulls on her dress, is leaving running fleeing, is at the door, and stops.

For he is not pursuing: he is simply lying there, watching, waiting, in wait. For her to choose. It is up to her to seize at last, for good, this one and only chance at singularity, at saving grace. She reaches for the door, pauses. Everything can be, will be, hers, it is true. But only if she—for she was never *she* at all, she understands, never a discerned or rarified *her*—chooses an existence both realized and obliterated. Yes. Only if she

    a) is a dead woman

    b) is a dead woman

    c) is a dead woman

ACKNOWLEDGMENTS

Thank you to the editors of the magazines, periodicals, and anthologies in which many of the stories in this collection first appeared, sometimes in earlier versions: *Tin House*, "Ball" and "The Knitting Story"; *Mississippi Review*, "Staples"; *Black Clock*, "Apology"; *Nerve.com*, "Bakery Girl;" *The Santa Monica Review*, "Fish"; *TriQuarterly*, "Needles."

In addition, "Wig" appeared in *Getting Even: Revenge Stories* (Serpent's Tail Press, 2007); "Musical Chairs," as "Timing," appeared in *Lost on Purpose: Women in the City* (Seal Press, 2005); "Cactus" appeared in *Another City: Writing from Los Angeles* (City Lights Books, 2001); and "Ball" appeared in *Bestial Noise: The Tin House Fiction Reader* (Tin House Books/Bloomsbury, 2003).

Thank you as well to the generous friends and mentors who offered critical feedback on these stories, and to the extraordinary Dan Smetanka, for his wisdom, vision, guidance, and patience.

ABOUT THE AUTHOR

Tara Ison is the author of the novels *The List, A Child out of Alcatraz*, a Finalist for the *Los Angeles Times* Book Prize, and *Rockaway*, featured as one of the "Best Books of Summer" in *O, The Oprah Magazine*, July 2013, and the essay collection, *Reeling Through Life: How I Learned to Live, Love, and Die at the Movies*.

Her short fiction, essays, poetry, and book reviews have appeared in *Tin House, The Kenyon Review, The Rumpus, Nerve. com, Black Clock, TriQuarterly, PMS: poemmemoirstory, Publishers Weekly, The Week, The Mississippi Review, LA Weekly*, the *Los Angeles Times*, the *San Francisco Chronicle*, the *Chicago Tribune*, the *San Jose Mercury News*, and numerous anthologies. She is also the co-writer of the cult movie *Don't Tell Mom The Babysitter's Dead*.

She is currently Associate Professor of Fiction at Arizona State University. Learn more at www.taraison.com.